THE OC

THE WAY BACK

SCHOLASTIC INC.

New York Toronto London Auckland Sydney
Mexico City New Delhi Hong Kong Buenos Aires

No part of this work may be reproduced in whole or in part, or stored in a retrieval system, or transmitted in any form or by any means, electronic, mechanical, photocopying, recording, or otherwise, without written permission of the publisher. For more information regarding permission, write to Scholastic Inc., Attention: Permissions Department, 557 Broadway, New York, NY 10012.

ISBN 0-439-67702-5

12 11 10 9 8 7 6 5 4 3 2 1   4 5 6 7 8 9/0

Cover and interior designed by Louise Bova
Printed in the U.S.A.
First printing, December 2004

1

Dear Mom and Dad,
No sarcasm — I'm gone. Are you standing? Sitting? Here goes . . .

Newport was silent. The Cohen home was quiet. The Cooper house had been sold. And the pool house was empty. As the sun rose over Orange County, the silence radiated. Seth Cohen, Marissa Cooper, and Ryan Atwood had gone their separate ways.

A year ago Newport held nothing for me. I was all alone.

Ryan Atwood had come to Newport hoping to find a family. A home. And for the last ten months he had lived in the Cohens' pool house. The Cohens, Sandy, Kirsten, and Seth, had become his family. And Newport was his home.

Before Ryan, I was, let's be frank, a loser.

Seth Cohen had spent his entire life trying to escape Newport. Friends had always been few and far between. But when Ryan entered Seth's life, everything changed. He had a brother, a friend. He was no longer alone.

I can't go back to that. If I have to be alone, I'm doing it on my terms. In my boat. On the open water where there are no limits.

Marissa Cooper had lived in the Newport spotlight for years. She was all things Orange County. She was gold and she was lovely. But Marissa wanted to escape, and when Ryan entered her life she found her way out.

I've lost the sarcasm. The wit. The Cohen charm. I am Sal Paradise. Out on the road. Out on the sea.

But everything changes. Over the year the three found themselves battling the boundaries of love and friendship and brotherhood. They were not likely friends, but their bonds had become strong and they were ready for all that life could throw at them — except this.

A new life. A baby.

And now, the three unlikely friends found themselves worlds apart from one another.

I can't imagine my life in Newport without a friend, a brother. That's why I'm leaving.

Ryan was back in Chino, sleeping on his friend Theresa's couch. Theresa and Ryan had been friends since childhood and in high school they had become more than friends. But it had always been more off than on. Then Theresa came to Newport to escape her fiancé, Eddie, and for one night she and Ryan were together. But now that night loomed over everything. Theresa was pregnant. The baby could be Ryan's. He had to take responsibility and start his own family.

Taking life's reins in my own hands. Grabbing control. A giant leap in a single bound.

When Ryan left, Marissa understood why he felt that he had to go, but it didn't mean that she didn't miss him. Now that Ryan was gone, she didn't have an escape. She was living with her mom and her new stepdad, Caleb Nichol, who was also Seth's grandfather. And she was drinking again. She drank to get drunk. Her only escape.

Not a leap of faith, but a real leap. And I'm ready.

Seth couldn't stay in Newport any longer. Without Ryan he felt weak, as if the forces of the city could take him down at any moment. He had to experience life on his own. Discover the real Seth Cohen. So he had set sail on his boat, the *Summer Breeze*, and hadn't looked back. Sailing far away from Southern California and a world he'd always wanted to leave.

Newport was not the same. The sun hovered over the bay and Balboa Island, warming the summer air, but Newport was cold. And each of the friends was alone. Waiting . . .

I promise to call. Write. Send a message in a bottle. I love you.

Seth

2

As the dusty sun rose over Chino, Ryan lay on the couch in Theresa's living room. He turned on the television, flipping through the channels, but there wasn't much on except for the news and infomercials at this early hour. It was five A.M. He had to be at work in an hour.

He flipped the channel again as he began to fold his blankets. A rerun of *The Valley* came on. Ryan laughed, remembering how Summer, Marissa's best friend, had been so obsessed with the show that she had gotten them invited to the star's party in L.A. That was right about the time he and Seth had discovered that Marissa's mother was sleeping with Luke, Marissa's ex-boyfriend. Ryan remembered how he had tried to take Marissa to L.A. so that Luke could break it off with her mom. Of course, Marissa discovered the truth anyway, but at least he had tried. Sometimes he wished that the only thing he had to worry about was Marissa and her problems, but he had much bigger problems now.

He was back in Chino, working and sleeping on

Theresa's couch. Back to what he had left just a year ago. But now things were complicated. There was Theresa and the baby. The baby that might or might not be his. And there was the fact that Ryan and Theresa had been best friends since they were kids and even boyfriend-girlfriend, but they were none of those things now. They were just here. In Chino. Two teens. A baby.

Ryan finished folding up the blankets, placed them in the hall closet, and pulled out a fresh T-shirt and jeans for work that day. He went into the bathroom to change and brush his teeth. He could hear Theresa stirring in her room.

He winced at the thought of waking her. Over the last few weeks Theresa had pushed him away, blaming it on her pregnancy and the summer heat. But Ryan knew the truth. They were both nervous and scared — and unprepared. Both sweating the fears of the new family they were about to become. The family neither had expected to have.

Ryan spit toothpaste into the sink and rinsed his mouth and his face. *Another day on the job*, he thought as he looked at his image in the mirror, *another day in Chino*.

In the kitchen, Theresa's mom had prepared breakfast — toast and cereal. Out of habit, Ryan went straight to the cupboard to look for fresh bagels or a better selection of cereal, but quickly caught himself — this wasn't his home. He had done this often, but always remembered that this wasn't the Cohens' kitchen. There was no selection.

He went back to the table, grabbed a piece of toast, and poured himself a bowl of generic wheat cereal. As he sat quietly eating his breakfast, Ryan thought about how drastically his life had changed over the past year. He had gone from living in Chino with his drunken mother and her angry boyfriend, to juvie, to a weekend at the Cohens', to a deserted home in Chino, back to the Cohens', and now back to Chino in a new home. And soon he'd have a new family. Theresa would give birth to the baby and whether or not it was biologically his, Ryan had accepted responsibility as the father.

Ryan took a bite of his cereal. It was stale and unappealing. He set down his spoon. He missed Seth and his morning ritual. He missed the Cohens. But he had an obligation. A promise and a responsibility.

He returned to eating his cereal.

"Do we have any pickles?" Theresa asked, entering the kitchen.

"We ran out," Theresa's mom started. "Have some orange juice. It's better for the baby."

Theresa looked at Ryan. On cue he got up and poured her some juice. She took the glass and slowly sipped it, but almost immediately she ran over to the sink and vomited. Morning sickness. She had it bad.

Ryan held her hair back as she cleaned her face with cool running water. "Told you I wanted pickles," she said, grabbing a paper towel.

"Theresa, I don't have time to go to the store today," her mother said as she started to clear Ryan's cereal bowl from the table. "You'll have to wait."

Theresa grabbed her stomach and turned to the sink. Ryan watched as she vomited once again. He winced at the sound. "I can pick some up on the way home," he said, hating to see her in this much pain.

Theresa turned to him, wiping the sweat from her forehead and the water from her eyes. "Can you get some ketchup, M&M's, and a box of Krispy Kremes, too? Maybe some chips? Want to rent a movie, too? It's Friday night," she pleaded, a smile finally crossing her face.

Ryan hesitated, thinking about the doctor bills they had to pay. "We don't have any mo —" But he stopped himself. He wasn't going to argue. He'd find the money. "Sure."

Theresa winked at him and headed to the living room to lie on the couch and relax.

Sweat poured down Ryan's forehead as he lifted wood beams onto a pallet and pushed them over to the construction site. He had spent the last month working with a crew to build a new house. When Ryan returned to Chino, he'd realized that he'd have to get a job if he was going to take on the responsibility of Theresa and her baby. And so he'd called Kirsten Cohen and asked her if she knew of any contractors in the area that might need help. And, Kirsten had been more than willing to help Ryan — the boy she regarded as her second son. And that was when Ryan heard the news that

Seth had gone . . . that Kirsten had lost both her boys.

After Ryan had started working, he called to thank Kirsten for the job and learned that Seth had ended up in Portland, Oregon. Ryan was shocked but knew that Seth would make it. Over the last year, Seth had gained a confidence Ryan had never seen in him before. He thought that his brother would be just fine on his own.

Ryan unloaded the beams in front of the house and started carrying them up to the second floor.

"Hey, Atwood. Drop 'em over here," one of the workers, Jose, said.

"Hey, you hear?" Jose asked as Ryan dropped the beams.

Ryan shook his head no.

"You might want to pick up the pace there. Apparently the big guy's been here all week. Watching us."

"So?" Ryan said, wiping sweat off his face.

"So? Rumor is, he likes what you're doing, ya get more money. And today's payday."

"Oh," Ryan replied, trying not to get too excited. He needed the extra money. Theresa was due in about six months and with all her cravings and the money he'd spent on doctors and preparations for the baby, he didn't have much in savings.

Ryan walked back downstairs and started carrying the beams four at a time up the stairs instead of the regular two at a time. The work was hard and his body was weak and hot and dehydrated. But he kept telling himself that each grueling step in the hot summer sun was another step closer to a bigger paycheck at the end of the day.

He took off his shirt and wiped the sweat from his arms. His newly buffed body glistened in the dusty sun as he worked right through lunch. He had a family to support.

Ryan watched some of his coworkers' wives and girlfriends come and visit them during the break as he continued to work. He thought about the families he once had — here in Chino and away in Newport. How he had gone from having no one and nothing to the Cohens', where he had it all. A bed of his own and more important, he had a mother, a father, and a brother. All the things he had always hoped his life in Chino would bring him, but never had. And now as he continued to sweat and work through lunch he thought about the new family he was about to begin. He would be the head of this family. He would have to be the father and support the mother and give the child love — all the things he had never had growing up.

Ryan worked until the sun disappeared. He was one of the last workers to leave for the night. He packed up his tools and made his way to the foreman's truck, where he picked up his paycheck.

"Thanks," he said as the foreman handed him his envelope. He walked over to his bike and opened the envelope. He pulled out the check and looked at the amount. There was no bonus. No extra money.

After a hard day at work, Ryan felt defeated. He folded the check and placed it in his pocket.

"Atwood," Ryan heard someone yell from behind him. He turned around slowly. It was Jose. "Hey, we're going to the pool hall. Grab a couple beers. Play a few games. Spend our bonuses. You coming?"

Ryan placed his hand on his pocket. He could feel the check inside it. Empty, without a bonus.

"Uh . . ." Ryan hesitated. He wanted to go. Spend all his money, be reckless for once this summer, but he couldn't do it. If he did, he'd be just like his father. And his mother. He couldn't spend the money he made on alcohol. It had been the ruin of his own family, and he couldn't make it the ruin of his new one. "I can't. I got to go home to Theresa. You understand?"

"Yeah, next time, man. I know how the ladies get when they want their man."

Ryan smiled. "Sure." And Jose walked away. *Sure*, Ryan thought, *if it were only that simple.*

He hadn't told the guys about his situation. About how Theresa was pregnant, about how he slept on the couch. All they knew was that he lived with her. As far as they were concerned, he was in a happy relationship with a beautiful girl.

It was times like these that Ryan wished Seth were around. He needed a brother, someone to help him cope with the pressures. But he didn't even know how to get ahold of Seth. And he wasn't sure Seth would want to talk to him. Actually, he was sure that Seth wouldn't want to talk to him. They had parted on pretty bad terms. Seth hadn't understood why Ryan had to leave. He hadn't understood that Ryan left for Theresa. That he hadn't abandoned his friend, his brother. That he had tried to do what was right. And he hoped one day Seth could understand, but now as he stood here in Chino, he started to doubt whether or not he would ever see his brother again.

Ryan hopped on his bike and rode home, saddened by the day, by the bonusless check and the memories of what he'd had. All he wanted to do was lie on the couch and rest. But as he neared the house, he remembered that he had promised to pick up some snacks and a movie.

So he turned around and rode back a few miles until he got to the strip mall that stood on the dusty street. He went to the ATM to deposit his money. But the machine was broken and wouldn't accept his card. Ryan pounded the machine, but still nothing happened. He was pissed. He had no money and he had promised Theresa.

He sat down on the sidewalk and thought about giving up, taking his bike and riding away, but the thought of another kid in the world without a father made him sad. Across the street the Cambio Money Exchange's lights were still on. And even though he knew that it would end up costing him money to get money, Ryan had to do it. He didn't want to disappoint Theresa.

In the Cambio, Ryan handed his check to the woman behind the safety glass and steel bars. She smiled at him and said, "This transaction will cost ten-fifty. Would you like an advance on your next paycheck? We can give you a discount."

"No, thanks," Ryan replied, remembering when his mom used to get advances on her paychecks when they had no money. Then she used it all for tequila and beer. She was always in debt. "This is fine," he said as the woman twirled the silver tray back out to him and he took his money.

Back on the other side of the street Ryan made his way into the small grocery store. He wandered aimlessly up and down the aisles. Trying to remember what he was looking for — all that he had promised Theresa.

He found himself in the baby aisle. Diapers. Bottles. Food and lotion. *How could one person demand an entire aisle for their survival?* Ryan thought as he wandered down the aisle. One day soon, he would have to shop in this aisle every week. He paused and looked at the diaper section. Forty diapers for twelve dollars. How would he ever make it? At this pace he'd never have enough money to support Theresa and the baby. Ryan started to panic and ran toward the frozen foods section.

From the giant freezer, he grabbed a gallon of ice cream and held it tight against his chest, trying to make his heart slow. Trying to numb his fears. And again he thought about the life he'd had in Newport. About Marissa. About how all he wanted to do was walk down the pier eating Balboa Bars, talking about school and parties and meaningless things that kids his age were supposed to talk about. He walked toward the candy aisle and picked up a bag of M&M's. Again, he thought of Marissa, how she would pull out all the green M&M's and eat them one by one. How much fun they could have together. How much fun they had together. But there was Theresa, he thought, and he couldn't desert her. Even if the baby wasn't his.

He held the M&M's tightly and walked toward the bakery aisle, where he found a box of doughnuts. Stale Krispy Kremes. And he shook his head. He picked up the box and held it under the bag of chocolates. The smell of old doughnuts enveloped the air in front of him — at least they were on sale now.

At the checkout counter Ryan handed the clerk the money from his pocket.

"Someone's having a party tonight," the clerk started. "Or PMS. For your girlfriend?"

"Yeah," Ryan said. He didn't have the time or the energy to explain. Theresa wasn't his girlfriend. And it wasn't PMS. She was pregnant. And the child might not be his. But he couldn't explain. He couldn't drag the clerk into the mess that had become his life again. He had to do this on his own. Ryan grabbed the bags of snacks, but paused when he saw the display of cigarettes at the front of the store, just steps from the counter.

"Can I get a pack of lights?" he turned and asked.

"Sure," the clerk answered. "ID, please."

Ryan hesitated. He wasn't eighteen and he'd never shopped here before. How could he have forgotten that he couldn't buy cigarettes here? That he had to go to the next town over, like he used to do.

He forced a smile at the clerk and said, "Never mind. Bad for you anyways." The clerk glared at him, scolding him for trying. But he wasn't about to let her get the best of him. "My girlfriend's pregnant," he said as he picked up his bags. "Bad for the baby." And he quickly walked out of the store. For the first time since he had arrived at Theresa's, he really felt in over his head. He was going to be a father. An adult. Yet he wasn't even old enough to buy cigarettes.

He went to the video store and returned home to Theresa with a forced smile on his face.

"Theresa," Ryan yelled when he got through the front door. "I'm —" But Theresa's mom came running out and put a hand over his mouth.

"She's sleeping."

Of course, Ryan thought, *it was almost nine o'clock and lately Theresa had been going to bed really early.* "Right," he said and walked over to the kitchen to put away the groceries.

But he didn't want Theresa to be asleep. He wanted to talk. Spend time with her like they used to as kids. So he quietly crept into her room and sat next to her on the bed.

"Hey," he whispered as he gently brushed the hair from her face.

Theresa twisted and slowly opened her eyes with a smile. "Hey," she replied.

"I stopped at the store. Got everything you wanted."

"You did?" She smiled again. He nodded. "Pickles," she said excitedly as she shifted her body weight and sat up in bed, moving toward him.

But Ryan retreated and his face went blank. He had forgotten the pickles.

"Pickles. Right," Ryan said softly. "I have to go back."

Theresa sat back in her bed. "Thanks."

And Ryan touched her hand as he left for the store once again. It was Friday night and all he wanted to do was relax. But he couldn't. He had a responsibility. A new life to look after. A child.

3

"Coop, are you awake? C'mon, get up."

Marissa awoke to a voice at her door.

"Coop, it's, like, six at night. Why are you still sleeping?"

Marissa stood up groggily, pushing her hair off her face. With Ryan gone, she had spent a lot of time in her room. Sleeping. Hiding. Avoiding the world.

"I was just . . ." She hesitated, not wanting to show Summer how weak she was. "Unpacking. I got tired, I guess."

Summer looked at her best friend quizzically, but moved to her closet, ready to throw clothes at Marissa and get her ready to go out, only to notice that it was empty and the room was a disaster.

"We got to get out of here," Summer said.

Marissa looked at her hesitantly — what was wrong with her room?

"Come on, this place is . . . Never mind. I have to get out. I've been reading Cohen's letter again," Summer reiterated.

"Where we going?" Marissa asked, not sure she wanted to leave.

Summer took one last look at the room. "Anywhere but here."

Marissa and Summer walked down the pier eating Balboa Bars. It had been a while since Marissa had been down here. She had spent the last few weeks drinking and hiding in her room or lying out by Caleb's pool. Summer had gone on vacation with her father during the first few weeks of summer and had just returned last week to find her friend in this state. They had spent the last few days hanging around Caleb's house, but hadn't really ventured into the Newport that they used to control.

"Have you talked to Ryan lately?" Summer asked.

Marissa let the cold of the chocolate melt in her mouth. She hadn't talked to Ryan since the first week he had gotten to Theresa's. They had tried to keep in touch but soon both had realized that they couldn't do it. They had to move on. And they decided, should their paths cross in the future then maybe they could try to be friends, but until then, it was just too hard. Ryan had a new life, and two other people to look after. She couldn't ask Ryan to look after her, too.

Marissa swallowed the ice cream. "No," she replied. She hadn't told Summer about her and Ryan's decision.

"Well, at least you know where he is," Summer

said. Marissa nodded. "And you could call him if you wanted."

"Yeah," Marissa said, even though she knew this wasn't true.

Summer licked her ice cream and sat down on a bench at the end of the pier. Marissa sat next to her and they watched as sailboats crossed in front of them, gliding over the cool water of the Pacific Ocean. Dolphins followed in their wake, seeming to smile at the girls.

Summer watched the boats pass and the dolphins wave good-bye with their smooth dorsal fins. "Who leaves a note?" Summer pondered aloud. "What is he? Like in 1980? The boy has a cell phone."

Marissa took another bite of her ice cream. The cold whispered in her mouth.

"Did he tell you where he was going?" she asked.

"No. Where have you been the last week? He set sail. The ocean is huge. It covers like three-quarters of the world. As far as I know, he could be in Tahiti or Fiji or some exotic place with beautiful women swarming all over him."

"Cohen with beautiful women?" Marissa asked with a laugh.

"Hey, I take offense to that."

"Sorry," Marissa said softly.

"Coop, what's up with you lately?"

"Nothing," Marissa replied. Lately, she'd lost interest in things. With Ryan gone, and Marissa living in Caleb's mansion with her mother, she just didn't

19

care. If it wasn't good news, she didn't want to hear it. She was tired of hearing about Summer and Seth, and worrying about Ryan and Theresa.

Summer finished her ice cream and tossed the stick in the trash as she stood up from the bench. Marissa sat, eating her Balboa Bar.

Summer paced, watching several more boats set out for an evening sail. She looked at Marissa, who sat absentmindedly watching the boats pass in front of her. "You know what I think," she began, snapping Marissa out of her daze. "I think we need to throw ourselves back into our old lives. We were fun before Cohen and Chino showed up. We went out, we did things. We didn't walk around the pier eating ice cream wondering when some guy would call or come back from his sail around the world."

Marissa took the last bite of her ice cream and put the rest in the trash. "Like what?" she asked, not sure she even wanted to know.

"I don't know. I just . . . aren't you bored?" Summer asked. The sailboats faded into the orange sunset on the horizon.

Marissa nodded yes. She was bored, but what else was there for them to do? Hang out at the beach and watch Luke's old friends surf? Go shopping? Hang out at the Fun Zone? She'd done these things since she was a kid. She was bored with it all. She wanted out of Newport. She wanted her escape. She wanted Ryan back.

Marissa stood up and joined Summer in her pacing.

But Summer had become restless and started walking down the pier, back toward the boardwalk. Marissa followed, and they walked in silence. Thinking. The sun was setting around them. The orange turning to gold and red and purple. The light of the day fading into the stars of the night. But they didn't notice. They could feel the other's thoughts. Newport wasn't the same without Ryan and Seth.

The ride back to Caleb's house was silent except for the music playing on the radio. The mansions and the palm trees and the groomed green grass of Newport passed by their windows. Uninviting. And when Rooney's "sh-sh-shakin'" came blaring over the speakers, both girls looked at each other. They knew. The pain. The reminder of their exes and even Oliver, who had turned out to be a psychopath. Summer shut it off.

"I hate that song," Marissa said. "It reminds me too much of —"

"That's it, Coop. Look at us. We're pathetic. I'm picking you up tomorrow morning and we're going to the beach. We'll take it easy. Ease back into our old lives slowly."

Marissa smiled okay as Summer stopped at the top of Caleb's driveway. But she wasn't sure she was ready. Not yet.

"See you tomorrow?" Summer asked as Marissa opened the car door. Marissa forced herself to nod yes. She had to. She had no excuse.

As Summer drove away and Marissa walked up

the long driveway to the house that she could not call her home, she thought about what Summer had said earlier on the pier. Were they really fun before Seth and Ryan showed up? Or were they just pretending? Marissa couldn't help but feel like their old lives weren't as glamorous as everyone had always made them out to be. Actually, she knew they weren't. She knew that Newport wasn't perfect. That their lives weren't perfect. That as soon as anyone pulled back the Orange curtain, they saw behind the artifice to the imperfections, the lies, the torment. Marissa wasn't ready to go back to that. She didn't want to become part of the facade again. She didn't want to be Newport. She didn't want to be perfect or imperfect. She just wanted to be herself.

As she approached the door of Caleb's mansion, she thought about running away. She had spent the last few years trying to escape Newport, and the only thing that had taken her away was Ryan. And now he was gone.

Sadly, Marissa entered the house, its large stillness echoing the emptiness she felt in her life.

"Mariss? Is that you?" her mom, Julie, called from the kitchen.

Marissa didn't answer, trying to escape up the stairs. Since she'd moved into Caleb's house, she'd done all she could to avoid her mother.

"Mariss, come eat with us. Caleb picked up some soup and sand dabs from the Crab Shack on his way home," Julie called.

But Marissa didn't feel like pretending tonight.

Pretending to be a family. Pretending to like Caleb. Pretending to believe that Julie was the perfect mother. Pretending to be happy. "I'm not hungry," she replied and quickly ran up the stairs to her room.

As she closed the door behind her, she thought about how so much had changed in her life over the past year. How she had gone from being the queen of the city, the heart of Newport, to an outsider. And how she had enjoyed every minute of it. How she had become comfortable being just Marissa. Dating Ryan, the true outsider, and easing away from all of the duties of being Newport, the social chair position, the crown of the homecoming queen . . . she had escaped them all.

Last summer, Marissa had been with Luke Ward, her boyfriend since the fifth grade. Even though they weren't always happy, they appeared perfect to the outside world, and she had thought that this was how life was supposed to be. But then she had met Ryan and she had finally found her escape.

Marissa sat down on her bed and looked at all the unpacked boxes and pictures leaning against the walls. Her room was a disaster, a mirror of her life. She took it all in and remembered when Seth and Summer had transformed her old room at her father's apartment into a foreign fantasy. They had put away all her things and painted a mural of Paris on her wall. They'd made her room a home.

Marissa stood up and walked over to one of the boxes where she had stashed the supply of alcohol that she had amassed over the summer. Stealing a bottle here and there from Caleb or her mom, left-overs from their parties. Sneaking bottles from any-where she could. Tonight, she wanted to run away, but as she brought the vodka to her lips she paused and thought about how much happier she had been once her room was put together. She placed the bottle back in the box and started wandering around her room. Contemplating. She could do this on her own. She needed this. Even if Caleb's house was not her home, she could at least make this room her own. And she could hide here.

In the corner, Marissa found a garment box full of dresses. She slowly opened it and discovered what was now a muddied past. Her cotillion gown. Her Missoni dress from the charity event on Caleb's yacht. And the Pucci dress, the symbol of her escape, the one thing she had held onto, and the one thing she had let disappear into her closet as Ryan entered her life.

Slowly she hung each dress inside her large walk-in closet. Each a reminder of her past. Each a symbol of the life she led last year. As she held the white cotillion gown in her hands she saw the faint stains of brown on the back edges that the dry cleaner had been unable to remove.

And she remembered that night. The night of her debut into Newport society. The night her dad had been knocked unconscious by Mr. Fisher over the financial mess that had caused him to lose his job, and the night she and Luke had broken up for the first time. And she remembered running. Running out onto the golf course, into the dewy green grass, and collapsing into the sand traps, grasping at her childhood, for a time when she felt safe in the world, a time when her father was her hero, her protector. And even now as she attempted to make sense of her life and her new home, she wondered if she'd ever feel those things again.

Her thoughts were interrupted by her mother at the door, gazing into her room, ready to yell, but calming when she noticed that Marissa was finally unpacking.

"Oh, Marissa, you're finally moving in," she sighed, stepping into the room.

"Yeah," Marissa answered softly.

Julie walked over to Marissa, who was still holding the cotillion gown.

"Your gown," Julie started as she grabbed the white dress from Marissa's hands and held it up close to her own body, as if she had once worn it. "You were so beautiful that night. Remember?"

Marissa nodded. Was her mom finally trying to declare a truce?

"Everything was perfect," Julie continued. "Well, except for the fact that your father was a lying, money-stealing thief and got himself knocked out," she started, then paused. "But that's all behind us. We have Caleb now. And this castle. And . . . you know what? We should go shopping someday. Like old times. We could go up to L.A. Hit Fred Segal, do lunch at Barney Greengrass, get massages at Burke

Williams. . . ." Julie continued on, psyching herself up for a trip Marissa knew would never happen, and Marissa continued to hang up her clothes. "It would be great," Julie finished.

"Sure," Marissa responded from inside the closet, not wanting to face her mother.

Julie walked into the closet and hung the gown next to the other dresses. Marissa kept her back to her mother, still scared of entering this family, lest she get sucked into the fantasy her mom was trying to present.

"Why don't you come downstairs and eat with us?" Julie asked.

"I'm not hungry," Marissa replied. She couldn't do it.

"Marissa," her mom said sternly. "Caleb went out of his way to get dinner for us. So we could eat like a family. And you will —"

"Fine," Marissa quipped. She was too tired to fight back, to hold strong and resist.

In the kitchen, Marissa sat across from her sister, Kaitlin, flanked on each side by Julie and Caleb. She really wasn't hungry, so she silently pushed the soup back and forth with her spoon, causing a tiny little wake of clams in the white creaminess of the chowder. Everyone was silent.

"Marissa," Julie started, trying to ease the silence. "Did you see Kaitlin's mani-pedi?"

Kaitlin held up her hands and pushed her chair

back to reveal her toes. "They're both French," she said.

"Nice," Marissa responded, barely looking at her sister.

"Look at your sister," Julie added.

"I did," Marissa said, dropping her spoon in her soup, realizing that any attempt Julie had made at a family just moments ago meant nothing. "I said her nails look nice. What else do you want?"

"I want you to stop acting like every minute you spend here is torture. This is not a dungeon."

"Nope, just the House on Haunted Hill," Marissa whispered under her breath.

"I heard that, young lady. Apologize to Caleb."

"Sorry," Marissa said quickly, barely glancing at her stepfather.

"It's okay," Caleb responded. Marissa pushed back her chair and got ready to get up. Julie motioned for her to sit down, but Caleb stopped her. "Juju, let her go. She's spoiling the sand dabs. Can't we just have a peaceful dinner for once?"

Julie glared at Marissa, who stood still, in shock. Had her stepfather really blamed her for spoiling his meal? What about the fact that he had spoiled her life? Her happiness? What about the fact that she had only come to live in this house because Caleb had blackmailed her into it? Held her father's financial well-being in front of her and asked her to choose? Let Jimmy continue to live in poverty without a job, or move in with Caleb and Jimmy would get two million dollars? Caleb Nichol was not Marissa's favorite person. Marissa looked to her mother, giving her one last chance to prove that this family existed, to prove that Marissa was a part of it.

"Marissa, weren't you leaving?" Julie asked as she dished out another sand dab for Caleb.

"Yeah," Marissa answered quietly, walking away from the table. Caleb's whispers echoed behind her, pushing her out the door. Out of the family. Her mother had failed her and she was all alone.

Upstairs, Marissa returned to unpacking her things. Clothes. Books. Photos and frames. Her room slowly becoming a haven, a hideaway from the evils downstairs. As she came across a photo of herself with Ryan a tear formed in her eye. She missed him. She wished that he were here to hold her. To tell her that everything would turn out just fine. That she could escape this horrible house, this mansion that represented all the things that she had grown to dislike. Marissa set the photo next to her bed. It was the closest she would get to seeing him soon.

A tear rolled down her cheek.

She looked around the room, at the half-unpacked boxes, and started to cry. In her heart, she knew, this could never make her happy. That no matter how organized or decorative she made her bedroom, it would never be her home.

She sat on the bed, letting the tears fall. Her breath became shallow as she gasped for air.

Through her tears, Marissa looked into her closet.

28

The Pucci dress hung bright and bold against the white cotillion gown. And she remembered the day she had bought the dress. The day before Ryan had come to Newport. She had bought it as an escape. A way to become anyone other than the person everyone expected her to be. But she had never actually worn the dress anywhere but in her room. Once Ryan had entered her life, she hadn't needed a dress to help her escape, she had him.

Marissa wiped the tears from her cheeks. A thought erupted in her head.

She stood up and went to the closet. Maybe the dress could help. But as she pulled it over her head and danced around her room, she felt no different. She was still the same Marissa. Alone. The dress didn't have the effect it once did. Just a desperate feeling of trying to escape the traps of Newport, traps that she had fallen into once again.

And so she turned to the one thing that had helped her escape over the last few weeks — the thing that she had tried to avoid since Summer had returned — but as she let the stinging vodka drip down her throat she slowly felt better. Different. Not like the Marissa everyone expected.

And she continued to drink until she passed out in her bed, the picture of Ryan watching over her.

When she awoke, bright sun was coming through the French doors of her balcony. She got up and stumbled over the boxes, her Pucci dress still clinging to her slender body.

In a slightly drunken hungover haze, Marissa meandered to the doors and out onto the balcony. From here, she could see all of Newport, an expanse of possibility to many, a prison to her. Even in the warm summer breeze she felt trapped. A princess in her ivory tower, locked away forever.

Below, Caleb stood with the gardening and pool staff, barking out orders, and Marissa was again disgusted. How had this become her family? Marissa looked sadly at the staff, wondering if they, too, felt trapped, or if they wanted to become a part of her world. And as she stood staring, one of the young staff looked up at her and smiled. Marissa smiled back. He was gorgeous with tan skin and dark features.

He was everything that wasn't Newport.

She bounced her hair off her shoulders and mouthed the word "hello."

He mouthed the word back. She felt the world take over.

And she smiled, then slowly walked just inside her room. Her tiny body was still visible from below, and as the gardener watched, Marissa slowly took off the dress, before disappearing inside.

If she couldn't have Ryan, then maybe he could be her escape.

4

Seth Cohen finished tying up his boat for the evening and headed up the dock to where Luke was waiting for him in his truck. Once he'd sailed away from Newport, Seth had realized that he had nowhere to go, so he'd decided to call the only other person he knew. He'd been at Luke's ever since.

Luke Ward had been one of Seth's biggest enemies since he could remember. Not that Seth himself created any enemies, he had always just been a geek. Getting beat up after school, shoved into lockers, or having his shoes peed in by the water polo team, Seth had been the ultimate outsider. He had spent the majority of his life with his parents as his only friends.

But last summer, all that changed. Seth's dad, who was a public defender, had brought his work home one night. A boy Seth's age who'd gotten arrested for stealing a car with his older brother. Ryan Atwood. And after Ryan's mother had left him for the second time, Seth's parents, Sandy and Kirsten, assumed legal responsibility for him, and Ryan Atwood became a part of the Cohen family. Seth had a brother. A friend. A reason to stay in Newport.

But after Ryan left to be with Theresa, Seth had no reason to stay. Newport wasn't home if he didn't have his brother. So he left his parents and Summer a note and set sail on his boat, the *Summer Breeze.*

"Hey, man," Luke said as Seth hopped in the truck.

"Hey," Seth answered, closing the door behind him. Every day after work, after helping out in the marina washing boats, mending sails, and teaching lessons, Luke would swing by and pick Seth up after a day of kiteboarding. This had become their routine. "So, what's the plan for tonight?"

"Not much," Luke answered. "Dad and Gus are making dinner. BBQ. Then nothing after that. Just you and me, I guess. The guys all went up to Columbia Gorge to camp."

"Oh, right," Seth said, remembering that most of their friends had taken off for a few days. "Barbecue sounds good. Is Gus making his sauce?"

"Of course," Luke answered. "I'm starving."

"Starving? More like famished," Seth said, grabbing his stomach. "This work thing really takes a lot out of you."

"Yeah," Luke said out of habit, turning onto the small road that followed the water all the way back to his house, back to where Seth was living for the summer. "Actually, wouldn't know. Never really worked."

"Me neither. Except for Chester and a few sailing lessons. But this whole down-and-dirty, put-some-real-elbow-grease-into-it sort of work is starting to grow on me. You know, like this beard," Seth said, pulling at the barely there five o'clock shadow that he had been trying to grow for the last week or so. "I think, Luke, I am finally becoming a man. I have a job. I have a beard. What more do I need? A mortgage? Yes. You're probably right. But for now I'm renting."

But Luke didn't answer. Much of Seth's humor still went way over Luke's head, but he'd learned to just smile and take it all in. Seth laughed. He didn't care that Luke didn't get his humor, he just liked that he had someone who would listen to him.

Luke continued to drive as Seth connected the transmitter to his iPod so that he could play his music through the car stereo. Once the iPod was all hooked up, Seth scrolled through his playlists and found his favorite song of the moment. It was a rock melody that he had picked up from a local band. Seth had spent much of his free time this summer going to concerts at small local venues — coffee shops, indie bookstores, even afternoons in the park. The music scene here was great. And that was part of the reason why he had decided to come to Portland in the first place. He knew that indie-artist, guitar-playing, hippie types had made Portland their home, and he wanted to see if he could make it his home as well. This new way of life intrigued him and he had thrown himself into every aspect of it. If he was going to spend the summer away from his family, his brother, and the love of his life, he had decided that he would make it worthwhile. That he would become the person he'd always wanted to be.

Luke took a sharp right turn and threw Seth out of his daze.

"What the — ?" Seth asked, hanging onto the door handle.

"Burnside, man. The guys out in the water today were talking about it. Said that some of the local guys who had gone pro were coming back."

Burnside was one of North America's greatest urban skate parks. Several pro skaters had come out of the half pipes and rails that sat under the Burnside bridge and both Seth and Luke had always been intrigued.

"Thought we'd check it out," Luke said as he continued to drive.

"Sure," Seth said. He was curious to see the tricks these guys could pull. In the short time he'd been in Portland, Seth had heard his fair share of legends and stories from Burnside. Even though he had been skating most of his life, Seth was intimidated by the crowd that made it's way there every night.

Luke pulled up to the side of the bridge and they got out of the car and started walking down to the park. There were kids everywhere. Skaters in Volcom and tattoos. Punks with candy-colored mohawks. Goths in black. Preps in Lacoste. Hippies with dreadlocks. All united by their love and awe for the sport of skateboarding.

Seth and Luke sat down on a grassy patch that gave the best vantage point of the half pipe where guys were doing flips and 360s.

"Man," Luke said. "That's, like, rad. You ever try that, Cohen?"

"Nah," Seth answered as another skater launched himself into the air. "I skated in Newport. Remember?"

"Right," Luke said. "Not exactly Burnside."

Seth nodded, thinking about Newport. Home for the last sixteen or so years. Hell for the majority of his life. Newport had too many rules. No skateboarding on the pier. No fires on the beach. And most certainly do *not* be different. Seth grinned as he looked around at all the kids around him. The different clothes, the different colors of their hair, and yet they were all hanging out in one place. Seth couldn't think of one place in Newport that would have this much diversity and not end up with a clash of cliques. Even Seth felt comfortable here. Like he belonged. Like no matter how different he was, he could still hold a civil conversation and not end up in a fight.

"Cohen," a girl with a pink mohawk screamed from a distance. "You finally made it."

"Yeah." Seth grinned. This was Petey, a girl Seth had met several times at a bookstore downtown. "How are you?"

"Good. Glad you came. Isn't this like the most Zenned-out experience?" she said as she breathed in the air around her. "It's so beautiful. All of us.

One place." Petey sat down between Seth and Luke and crossed her legs in front of her, closing her eyes and placing her hands palms up on her knees.

Luke looked over at her and then gave Seth a look. Luke hadn't quite gotten the vibe of Portland yet and Seth could sense his uneasiness.

"What time were Gus and your dad expecting us, Luke?" Seth asked.

"Don't know, man. They're probably making out. They won't care."

Seth gave Luke a shocked look. Luke just stared back at Seth, what?

"Right. Sorry. Used to be funny when it was my mom and dad. Still getting used to the gay thing."

Seth just nodded okay, trying to make Luke feel comfortable again.

"Your dad's gay?" Petey asked, suddenly perking up from her Zen meditation state.

"Yeah," Luke said softly, waiting for the same sort of response he'd gotten in Newport. Waiting for the punch or the cruel joke.

"Cool," she said. "So's my mom. Kind of nice to have two of the best world, don't you think?"

"What? I guess," Luke responded, not quite sure what Petey was talking about.

"My favorite parent was always my mom. But now I have two moms. Two of the best world."

"Oh. Never thought about it like that," Luke answered, slowly opening back up to Petey, turning back toward her.

"That's because you haven't been hanging out with me," Petey said flirtatiously as she stood up and skipped back to her friends on the other side of the park.

"See, told you the gay-dad thing would come in handy one day," Seth said as he, too, stood up.

"No you didn't." Luke stood up, too.

"I didn't. Well, I meant to." Seth started walking back toward Luke's truck, the skaters still flying through the air behind him. "Let's go. I'm starving."

"Sorry we're late. Luke was flirting," Seth said as he walked into the Wards' kitchen with Luke trailing behind. Luke's dad was chopping up vegetables and preparing a salad while Gus was barbecuing outside.

"I wasn't flirting."

Seth picked up a couple of chips and tossed them into his mouth, then turned back to Luke. "What would you call that, Luke? A little eye-batting. The cautious look. That's not baseball." Gus appeared at the window. "Gus? Ruling?" Seth yelled out the screen.

"Flirting," Gus answered as he turned back to the grill.

"No fair," Luke said as he playfully tossed a chip at the screen. "No outside rulings."

"So, who's the girl?" Luke's dad asked as he finished preparing the salad.

"No one. Just a friend."

37

"We'll see," Seth snickered as he grabbed the salad and took it outside to the table.

"Ribs are ready," Gus yelled.

Outside, the sun had almost set on the waters of Portland. Small, calming waves lapped at the edge of the Wards' backyard. Seth and his new family, Gus, Luke's dad, and Luke, sat around the table eating their dinner, their faces covered in sauce from the ribs.

"Seth, you got another letter from your mom today."

Seth put down his fork. "Money?"

"What do you think?" Gus asked.

"Right. Well. You know what to do with it." Seth picked up his fork again and continued to eat.

"We can't keep taking your money," Luke's dad protested as he filled his mouth with salad.

"Think of it as rent. I'm staying here, eating your food. I'm not a cheap mouth to fill. I like tapioca pudding. The finer things in life. Seth Cohen does not come without a price."

Luke started laughing.

"Fine, but next time you keep the money," Luke's dad said, knowing that he wouldn't get too far with this argument. "You might need it for the trip home. I heard Greyhound's raised their rates. Very scary."

"Very funny." Seth laughed as he pushed his plate away from him, finished with his meal. "I sailed to Catalina. Santa Barbara. *That* was scary."

"Yeah, and then you called me from the bus station when you got to Portland," Luke chimed in to laughter.

"You haven't heard the stories. The adventures of Seth Cohen. I *am* adventurous."

"Indulge us," Gus said as he placed his napkin on the table and leaned back in his chair.

Since Seth had arrived in Portland he hadn't really told anyone his stories. He kind of liked the mystery and the idea that he had just randomly shown up. He liked the spontaneity it suggested and, if truth were told, part of him had always thought that no one would be interested. He had spent most of his life telling his stories and adventures to a plastic horse, Captain Oats. And no one, besides his parents — and even they got bored at times — had ever given him the audience he deserved. But now that he had lived in Portland for several weeks, that part of Seth Cohen was slowly disappearing. He was starting to feel that his opinion mattered. That people were actually interested in the things he had to say. Especially his new friends and family. And he didn't feel like he was just talking to indulge himself or a plastic horse, but that people were genuinely interested in discovering more about Seth Cohen.

Seth sat back in his chair and cleared his throat. All eyes were on him. He paused for a moment, thinking about how to begin, and then he started.

"So, there I was floating outside of the harbor. Just beyond the seals on the big buoy. You know the ones." The guys all nodded. "And the sun was golden orange. Reflecting off the water. A nice breeze. A few whitecaps. And I was sailing."

"Cohen, we didn't ask for the poetic version of *Moby-Dick*."

"Right. No poetics. No *Moby-Dick*." Seth paused. Confused. "What else is there to sailing the open sea? The wide-open water. The beauty of it all. The solitary happiness?"

"Uh, the chicks you banged, the booze you drank, the loot you stole," Luke chimed.

"It wasn't *Pirates of the Caribbean: The Adventures of Seth Cohen*, Luke."

"Right." Luke sat back in his chair, perplexed. "No chicks at all?" he tried once more.

Seth shook his head.

"Some guys do more than just think about girls," Gus said.

"Coming from a guy that sleeps in the same bed as my dad," Luke responded.

Gus and Luke's dad stared at Luke. Should they be mad or laugh that Luke could finally make a joke about their living together? The guys continued to stare. Seth finally broke the ice.

"Ah, the Cohen charm has finally started to wear off on him. I'm sorry. It happens. Should've seen Ryan."

"Ryan wasn't much of a talker," Luke said.

"Right. But you could see it in his eyes. That look. His brooding one. The head tilt to the side." Seth did an impression and Luke started to laugh.

"I bet he had a constant flow of witty banter running through his head. A slide show. Perhaps a full-length feature."

"Where is Ryan anyways?" Gus asked.

"I already told you," Luke started, trying to quickly change the subject, knowing that it was not a good one. Seth got suddenly quiet. "He went back to Chino."

"I forgot," Gus said, turning to Seth with an apologetic look.

Seth sat quiet for a moment, thinking about Ryan. How he had just abandoned Seth in Newport. Left him to fend for himself. Left him without a best friend, a brother. The anger slowly boiled up. He had been ignoring the subject all summer.

"It's okay," Seth started. "Who needs a brother anyways when I can make it all the way up to Portland and live with my two dads and Luke?" He quipped quickly, trying to change the subject. Trying to erase the pain. Turning back to laughter.

The guys started to laugh and joke around.

"So, really, how did you end up here?" Gus asked.

"Well, and please excuse any poetics, but the sea, it's just so lovely." Luke's dad and Luke looked at him with a smile. "Sorry. Couldn't help it. The rhyme is just too easy to pass up."

"The story, Cohen," Luke said.

"Right. So after Ryan left I decided that I needed a change. And what screams change more than getting the hell out of Newport? Nothing." Gus and

Luke's dad nodded in agreement. When they'd been discovered as a couple, they too had left Newport and moved to Portland to start over. "Knew you'd understand. So, since I didn't have a car, and I didn't want to steal one, I took my boat. Headed straight out from the harbor, but once the sun went down, I started to panic. The reality of what I'd done started to hit me. I'd kind of set sail in a hurry and I didn't really have a plan. So I curled up and fell asleep under the stars. Just drifting in the boat. I figured I'd just let the sea guide me. If I ended up back in Newport then I was supposed to be there for the summer, but if I ended up somewhere else then it was a sign to move on. So the next morning when the sun was beating on my face and the waves were crashing against the boat, I woke up to find myself slamming into a giant yacht with every surge. Well, I panicked. I was sure I was back in Newport. But when I looked around I realized that it wasn't Newport. I was on an island. I had made it to Catalina."

The guys giggled.

"One whole night, and you'd only made it to Catalina?"

"Yes. But obviously I wasn't supposed to be in Newport. So I set sail north, but when I reached Malibu the wind died and I had to hitch myself to another giant yacht and they took me all the way to Santa Barbara. That's when I decided the whole sailing-around-the-world thing wasn't going to work. Josh Slocum had one leg up on me and I wasn't about to test fate anymore."

"Who's Josh Slocum?" Luke asked.

"He sailed around the world alone. Wrote a book about it?" Luke just nodded cluelessly. "Never mind. Anyway. So I went to the bus station and asked how far they went north in the U.S. They said I could take a bus direct from there to Portland and hop on another bus to Seattle. And of course, I heard Portland and said 'one ticket, please.' Then I met Cali and she said we should stay in Portland, that it was better than Seattle. And she had a cute smile. And I knew you guys were here. So that's how I ended up at your doorstep. No great mystery. No chicks — okay, one. Booze. Loot. Just a small adventure, but I'm glad I did it."

"We're pretty glad you made it, too. Luke was starting to get lonely."

"Dad?!" Luke protested.

"What?" his dad said with a grin. "Admit it you were bored hanging out with us."

Luke just grunted.

The guys cleared the table and finished up the dishes as the lightning bugs flashed yellow outside the windows. A cascade of tiny stars falling within reach.

Seth looked outside and noticed the bugs flying about. He stepped back outdoors and watched as one landed on his arm. Its glow lit the hairs on his arm.

"I will never understand these things. No matter how long I live here," Seth said as he watched the bug fly away.

* * *

Later Seth lay wide awake, thinking about Ryan. And he couldn't sleep. He missed the nights when he and Ryan used to talk and recount their days together. He missed the brotherhood.

Seth's thoughts were interrupted by a knock at the door. It was Luke.

"So, do you really think she liked me?" Luke asked as he entered the room and sat at Seth's desk.

"Who?" Seth asked, unclear.

"The girl. Pink hair. I forget her name, but —"

"Petey?" Seth asked again, confused.

"Yeah." Luke looked at his hands and peeled the skin off the cuticles at the beds of his nails.

"You? Like Petey?"

"Well, I mean does she like me? 'Cause if —"

"Luke. You don't just like a girl because she likes you. You have to have a connection. A spark. Something to light the fire under the log of romance."

"Right. Sorry. Just starting conversation."

Seth sighed.

"It's like Summer and me. I always knew we had a connection. That spark. But I just had to wait for her to come around. And when she did? That's when things caught on fire. I didn't like her because she liked me. Granted, the obsession came when I was in third grade. But I had patience. And look what happened. She finally came around. When we had sex? It was beautiful."

"You —"

"Okay. It wasn't beautiful at first. It was awkward and weird, but we got through that phase and I think we both came out on top."

"You and Summer? Really?"

Seth nodded.

"I never would've guessed."

"What? That I was such a stud? Such a virile man?" Seth said, inflating his chest with pride.

"No. That she really loved you."

And Seth's chest fell. Luke had hit the nail on the head.

"Yeah, she did," Seth said softly, his demeanor slowly changing. He hadn't even said good-bye, just left a note.

"She was hot," Luke said. Seth glared. "Well, she was."

"I miss California girls sometimes. Blond hair. Tan. Blue eyes. Shaves. You know." Seth nodded but he wasn't really listening. His mind was on Summer. "Well, thanks for the advice. We going to go out sailing tomorrow with Cali?"

Seth sat quietly, not responding. "Oh, yeah."

"Aren't you guys sailing to Astoria next weekend, too?"

"Yeah."

"Hey, so what's with you two? You going to do her, too, now that the Cohen is such a stud?"

"No. We're just friends."

"Right."

"Well, see you tomorrow."

But Seth couldn't focus. His mind was on Summer. How he had abandoned her. The love of his life and he just left. The guilt set over him.

He was a horrible friend. Boyfriend. And Luke was right, she loved him and he just left her.

Seth picked up the phone and called Summer.

"Cohen?" she asked, surprised to hear his voice.

"Don't hang up." Seth sat down on his bed.

"Why? Because you don't have money to send a telegram. Where the hell are you?"

"I'm fine."

"Oh, great. Well, now I can sleep at night. Seth Cohen is safe and sound."

"I'm sorry, Summer," he whispered. Not knowing what else to say. He knew he should've come up with a better plan. A script for the phone call.

"You're not sorry. You just want to have some girl you can call up out of the blue after you left her a note and no good-bye."

"But I love you," he blurted without thinking.

"Stop."

"Please, I do. I know you love me."

"I can't, Cohen. You can't just leave me like that and expect things to be okay. You're probably not even coming back to Newport."

"I might. I don't know," he answered, not knowing what the future held in store for him.

"So you want me to wait around for you?"

"Is that bad?"

"Yes. You ass. I got to go."

"Summer, wait," he gasped, but he didn't have anything else to say. He didn't know what else to say.

"Don't call here again. I don't want to hear your Cohen voice." And with that, Summer slammed the phone down. Seth heard the crash. He knew that he had ruined things.

That it would take a lot of Cohen charm to get Summer back, if he ever returned to Newport.

5

The sun of Chino lay low in the sky as the long summer day came to a close. Ryan returned from work, his body sweaty and aching from the hot sun and the labor of constructing homes, to find Theresa on the porch waiting for him. Her dark hair was pulled back from her face and her belly protruded from within the confines of her little white sundress. Ryan smiled at the sight as he pulled up the driveway on his bike.

"Hey," he said as he laid the bike down in the gravel on the side of the garage.

"Hey," she replied, then motioned for Ryan to join her on the porch. Her small hands were swollen from the pregnancy. He smiled, then held up a finger, *one moment.*

He wiped the sweat from his forehead with his dirty T-shirt, then walked over to the spigot next to the porch and turned it on. The water flowed cold as he placed his hands under the stream, and he watched as all the dust and dirt and sweat of the day washed into the dried out grass of the yard.

Theresa sat watching. Waiting. And Ryan continued to let the cool water flow over his calloused and beaten hands, apprehensive. What was she waiting for? What had he done? His brow dripped more sweat and he splashed the cool water on his face. The wetness eased his fears for a second. Theresa had been on a rampage lately. Demanding this and that, and things had only gotten worse since the last time he had been sent out to get snacks and groceries. It seemed that no matter how hard he tried, he was always wrong and could do nothing right.

Finally Ryan turned off the water and joined Theresa on the porch. She put her hand on top of his. The coolness of the water radiated into her sweaty palms. He felt her take him in. His strength. Ryan looked at her. A smile inched across her face. She wasn't mad. Ryan smiled and she smiled back. Maybe he was wrong again.

"I miss this," she whispered quietly into the summer air, squeezing his hand tighter.

Ryan paused. Unsure. His hand slightly trembling beneath her firm grip. He wasn't sure if he could handle this. "Theresa, I don't know if this is such a good idea. You and me and the —" He placed his hand upon her stomach. "Are we really going to . . ."

Theresa gripped his hand tighter. "No," she said firmly and turned his face to look at hers. "This is not . . ." and she removed his hand from her belly. "This is not what I'm talking about."

Ryan pulled away. He could feel Theresa trying to pull him back. Desperate. Her eyes upon him, but he was confused. He looked at her and then his heart fell as he watched a tiny tear roll down her cheek.

"I miss you and me. As friends. Without this." She looked at her swollen stomach. "When we were free and young and innocent."

Ryan wiped the tear from her cheek.

"Don't you remember?" she pleaded, and Ryan nodded. He did remember. And he missed those times. He missed when she was his best friend. When they ran around the neighborhood together hiding from the police helicopters and pretending they were being chased, sleeping on her couch to avoid his mother and whatever drunk boyfriend she had brought over for that month. He missed smoking cigarettes with her and talking. He missed the surprises she left for him, the cigarette turned upside down — the lucky one. He missed her smile and her laugh. And he missed the two of them together with no complications.

He placed his hand upon hers. "I remember."

Then he thought about the night he had left her. The night he and Trey, his brother, had run off to a party and ended up stealing a car, attempting to escape from the hell that had become their lives. Chino.

"I'm sorry," he said.

"We both did this," she started but then caught herself. "Or there's a chance we did."

"I know." Ryan paused, then asked, "What if I hadn't gone to Newport?"

Theresa looked at him and he waited for her response. If he hadn't gone, none of this would have happened. He felt it. The guilt. The pressure of starting his own family. Would they still be friends if he hadn't left? She could've married Eddie and she never would have run away to him in Newport. His mind continued wandering. It was all his fault.

"Then you never would have met the Cohens. And you never would have had the life you deserve," she said, surprising him.

"But," he started, ready to accept the guilt. The blame.

"I'm sorry," she said. And another tear dripped down her cheek and another, her hormones and emotions overtaking her. "For being so mean. I know that you're trying. Sometimes this is just too much," she cried.

Ryan reached out and held her. Her body shook with sobs and his mind raced. He had to say something to help her, ease her pain.

"This is no one's fault. We can't beat ourselves up about this for the rest of our lives." He hugged her tightly, her swollen stomach pressing up against his. "You're my family. You always will be."

Theresa's body continued to convulse with fear, but Ryan held strong. He had to, he was the man of the house now. The father.

"Sleep with me tonight," she said softly between tears.

"Yes," he whispered and he held her tighter until the sun of Chino set and the darkness overcame the street. Then he helped her up and they walked to her room. Ryan tucked her into bed and went to the bathroom to shower off the exhaustion of his long day. And when he returned he expected to find Theresa asleep, but she was awake.

He climbed into bed next to her and they lay silent, the tips of their pinky fingers entangled in comfort.

"Do you really think this will work?" Theresa asked as she stared at the fan on the ceiling twirling round and round. Ryan watched the white blades of the fan repeat circles until they became one. Doubt filled his mind, but again he stayed strong.

"I'll make it work," Ryan answered.

Theresa leaned over and kissed him on the cheek. Ryan smiled and watched as she turned back around and let sleep overtake her.

As Theresa slept, Ryan's mind wandered. That night he'd reaffirmed his promise to Theresa that he would make this work. That no matter what, no matter whose baby it really was, he would take on the role of the father.

But as he lay in bed thinking, his hands and feet trembled with fear. He had never had a father. His own father had gone to prison when he was young. And the only other father he had known was Sandy Cohen, but he had only been with Sandy for a year before he had left to become a father himself. He was too proud to let someone else help, and he had convinced himself that he could do this on his own. But now as he watched Theresa sleep, he wasn't sure he would make it. If he could be the kind of father he had never had. He needed help.

Theresa stirred and whimpered, a bad dream. He touched her hair, its softness calming the tremble in his hand, and his touch calmed her fear. He thought about the prospect of being a father and it scared him, but after tonight, he thought, at least he and Theresa would be okay. And he fell asleep with the comfort of knowing that they had become friends again.

The next morning Ryan awoke to find Theresa gone. An indentation in the bed the only sign of their night, and the tremble returned to his hand. In the kitchen, he could hear Theresa and her mom arguing and Ryan knew this was not a good sign. Theresa was in another one of her moods. Another one of the moods where Ryan became the enemy and nothing he said or did could make things right. But he went into the kitchen with confidence. After last night, he felt like things had changed, that even though he wasn't sure how to be a father, he at least knew how to make things right with Theresa.

But as he entered the kitchen, his confidence was shattered. He had been wrong.

"I'm hot. I'm sweaty. It's all your fault," Theresa said as she held back her hair and splashed her forehead with cool water from the kitchen sink.

Ryan tried to go to her. But she held out her hand.

"I can't share a bed with you again."

"But, you, it was your . . . ," Ryan started, trying to get her to remember, to recognize that it was her idea.

"I know, but you should have known better. Gotten out of bed. I told you before it was too hot to sleep together."

"Sorry," Ryan said, trying again to comfort her.

But she backed away.

Ryan retreated and grabbed some fruit, then quickly went out the front door. He knew there was no use arguing. No matter what he said he'd be wrong, so he left for work and didn't look back. He'd have to find another way to make this work.

All day, as Ryan sat sweating under the hot summer sun, he thought about Theresa and his responsibility as a father. He couldn't concentrate. The menial task of hammering nail after nail into piece after piece of wood seemed so small and pointless in comparison to the greater aspects of his life — the prospect of being a father and having to raise a child. But Ryan continued to work. He and Theresa needed the money for the baby.

"Hey, Atwood," Jose called out to him. "What's with you today, man? Late night with the lady?" The other workers started making catcalls.

Ryan just glared the way he always did. His head turned to the side, brooding. "Yeah," he mumbled under his breath.

He still hadn't been able to tell the guys at work

about his situation at home. That he wasn't with his girlfriend, that he wasn't up late at night making out with her. That he was going to be a father. Instead, he continued to work through the rest of the day.

Lifting wood, hammering, and sawing, sweat dripping down his muscled body, he thought about being a father. And he thought about his family, Sandy and Kirsten and Seth, and wondered what they would say. Doubt filled his mind. Why did he always agree to help everyone else?

He wanted to call Seth and ask his advice. His help. Seth always had a plan for everything. No matter how small or big it was, Seth had a precise plan on how to get the job done, and right now Ryan felt like he needed one of those plans.

The summer sun continued to beat down on Ryan as he worked through the end of the day and through his thoughts. He couldn't help Theresa but even if things weren't good between them, he'd have to make it as a father. He wanted to do something right.

But, again, he needed a plan. And he thought about what Seth would say in the situation. How Seth would probably send him to see his own dad, Sandy, claiming he didn't know the first thing about being a dad, but he was sure a dad would know. And Ryan laughed at how ridiculous he had been, sweating and working through the day with the fear of fatherhood. All he had to do was ask Sandy.

* * *

Ryan returned home that evening with a plan. He would call Sandy and learn what it took to become a father.

After dinner, Ryan quietly crept into Theresa's brother's old room, and dialed the Cohens. The phone rang twice, then Ryan heard Sandy's voice greeting him.

"Ryan," he exclaimed, almost too excitedly. "Kirsten, it's Ryan." Ryan could hear Kirsten in the background sending her greetings.

"Hey," Ryan said shyly, not sure how to start the conversation. How to ask Sandy what it took to become a father.

"What's going on?" Sandy asked. "How's Theresa? Are you guys doing okay? Do you have enough money?"

Ryan paused and thought about answering Sandy's questions truthfully. He thought about telling Sandy that Theresa and he weren't getting along, that he was working twelve hours a day in the hot sweaty sun only to find that at the end of the week he barely had enough money to make it through the next week. But Ryan resisted and said, "Everything's fine. Theresa's good. A little moody, but aren't they supposed to be?"

Sandy laughed. "Good to hear."

A silent beat filled both telephone lines.

"Mr. Cohen?" Ryan started.

"Ryan, it's Sandy."

"Right. Sorry. Sandy, when Seth was . . . did you ever . . ."

56

"Get nervous?" Sandy finished for him. "Of course. But you'll learn. It just comes to you. And once they're here it's like having a puppy around. You clean up its poop. Feed it. Make sure it stays clean. It's easy."

Ryan thought for a moment, then answered, "I never had a dog."

"Oh," Sandy whispered, then paused.

"Or a father."

And the phone went silent again.

"I don't know if I can do this," Ryan finally said.

He could hear Sandy shuffling his feet on the other end. Thinking. Then he finally started talking.

"Ryan, if anyone can do this, you can. You're a smart kid. You have a future. So you ran into a little roadblock, but you'll get through it. Of every kid that ever passed through my office, you had the most potential. You know that. That's why we took you in. You're my son and no son of mine ever walks away from a challenge."

"But you were the only father I had," Ryan said. "And how will I know? Not to make the same mistakes as . . ."

"As your father," Sandy finished for him.

Ryan whispered, "Yes."

And again silence overtook the phone. Ryan thought about his own father. How he had gone to prison and how he had never really known him, just heard horrible stories from his mother. And he started to wonder what his father was like. A faint memory flickered through Ryan's thoughts. There had been a time when he and Trey and his mom and father used to be happy, but it was so distant that Ryan had a hard time focusing. Making it a concrete image. But he thought that if they were happy once, then there must have been something that made everything change. Something that had made his mother date a slew of men who abused her and made her drink until she was numb and oblivious to the pain around her. But what had been the impetus for this dramatic change? What had forced his father to turn against the law, against his family, and end up in prison? There had to be something. And now Ryan was entranced, interested. And he knew what he had to do. He had to find his father and ask him. He needed to know. What was it that had made their entire family fall apart?

"Ryan? Are you there?"

"Yeah. I was just thinking. There's something I need to do. Can you give me a ride somewhere on Saturday?"

"I'll be there at ten," Sandy answered without asking questions, without forcing Ryan to explain that he needed to go to the prison and visit his own father. That he needed to know the truth.

"Thanks," Ryan said as he hung up the phone.

And as he turned around to walk out of Arturo's room, he found Theresa standing in the doorway. Staring. He wondered how long she had been there, how much of the conversation she had heard.

But he didn't say a word and neither did she. They just stood there staring at each other. All their fears and doubts surfacing, boiling over. But neither said a word. Because they knew. Whatever it was they were about to embark upon, whatever fatherhood and motherhood entailed, they weren't really ready for it at all. They were only seventeen. They were still children. Ryan's thoughts flashed to his father. A glimmer of hope crossed his face. If only he knew the truth, then maybe somehow he could make this work. He looked at Theresa, who was holding her stomach. He had to make this work. He couldn't let this baby grow up in a family without love.

He stepped toward Theresa and placed his hand on her shoulder, then he looked into her eyes and whispered, "I promised you."

A tiny tear fell down her cheek and he walked away. He needed to become a father but first he needed to know what had failed his own, then he could mend his relationship with Theresa.

That Saturday, Ryan woke up early, before the sun had even peeked above the tiny homes of Chino. He couldn't sleep. All night he had tossed and turned, thinking about his father. The last memory he had. The memory of his father saying good-bye.

A small Ryan sat on his bed waiting. The house was cold and tiny and everything was damp with fear. Their family was being torn apart and Ryan could feel the pressure as if their house were being quartered, four horses with ropes pulling them in opposite directions.

A faint knock, then Ryan's door opened and his father stood there. Alone. Solemn. Without words. Ryan looked up at him. Frozen, but wanting to run to him and wrap his arms around his leg and never let go. A small child playing games. Only this game was for real. And Ryan couldn't act like a child. He was told he was a man and he needed to be strong. He wasn't allowed to let a tear fall. Atwood men did not cry. His father had ingrained this in him since he was a little boy.

Ryan sat still on his bed, his father looking at him. But Ryan held strong. He swallowed the tears and sat calmly. His father walked to him and held out his hand. Ryan looked down into it. And there across his rough and calloused skin lay a leather band. Just like the leather band his father had tied around his own neck. Ryan looked at his father, at the band, then picked up the band and proceeded to tie it around his own neck. The two looked at each other, each of their necks bound by a strap of leather. A father and a son. Then Ryan placed his tiny hand upon his neck and watched as his father disappeared without a word.

Ryan walked out to the front porch of Theresa's house and sat alone, swallowing tears as he thought about his father in prison and waited for Sandy to arrive.

The ride to prison started off silent except for the few directions Ryan gave as Sandy drove his BMW through the backstreets of Chino. Ryan still hadn't told Sandy where they were going.

They drove past graffiti-covered walls, dark and boarded-up stores, and dingy homes. Sandy's black BMW was out of place against the poverty and despair of the city. As they approached the freeway, Ryan broke the silence.

"I had to see him," Ryan said and looked out the window, hoping Sandy would recall their previous night's conversation.

Sandy paused in thought, then began, "Your father?"

"Yes."

Sandy nodded okay as Ryan continued to stare out the window, thinking. Wondering what to say to his father. Devising a plan. Then a moment of doubt surfaced — would his father even recognize him? Ryan's hands began to sweat. He wiped his palms across his jeans and held them up to the air-conditioning vents.

"Don't be nervous," Sandy said. "You'll be fine."

"It's been a long time."

"He'll remember," Sandy said with a look of comfort.

Ryan fidgeted with his sweaty palms some more. He wasn't comforted.

"We don't forget."

"You never met him," Ryan answered quickly.

"I didn't forget Seth."

"He left four weeks ago."

"A long time in the Cohen household. We're a close-knit bunch," Sandy said, smiling.

Ryan smiled back. An ounce of comfort entering him.

"How is he?"

"Seth?"

Ryan nodded.

"He went to Portland and moved in with Luke and his family."

"Luke?" Ryan asked, shocked.

"Apparently, he's trying to broaden his horizons. Discover the real Seth Cohen."

Ryan laughed. The thought of Seth and Luke living together was, well, not expected. Ryan couldn't think of two more completely opposite human beings on the planet. Sandy joined in his laughter. It was good to be back, Ryan thought. Even if he wasn't in Newport, he felt home again. Like a part of a family.

"How's Kirsten?" he asked.

"Good." Ryan looked at Sandy, *really*? "Okay, she's a wreck. Don't tell her I told you. She misses you guys. And Seth, in his quest to find himself, has decided he doesn't have much to say to her. They really haven't talked."

Ryan sat still for a moment. He felt bad. He had left with Theresa so quickly that he had never thought about the fact that he was leaving a family behind. That by starting his own family he was almost, in essence, destroying another family.

"I'm sorry," Ryan said quietly.

"It's not your fault. You did the right thing. You're *doing* the right thing. We understand. And I believe in you."

"Thanks." Ryan paused. "How are you doing?"

"Better now that I'm with my son."

Ryan and Sandy smiled at each other. And as they pulled up to the prison, Ryan had the confidence to make things right. To find out the truth about his father, to return to Theresa with the knowledge that he himself would be a good father.

Ryan sat behind the glass that separated the waiting room from the rest of the prison. His hands and heart shaking. His mind a blank. His father would appear soon and he still hadn't figured out what to say. Families and lovers, friends and lawyers, buzzed around him with hope, sadness, and despair. Ryan felt out of place. He had never been here before. Could he really do this? But he had to. If anyone would understand, it would be his father. He had convinced himself of this truth.

And if he ever expected to be a father himself, he needed to settle this once and for all. What had gone wrong between his mother and his father? Why had things gone sour between them? He had to know.

Ryan took a seat in his assigned booth. The chair was old and the plastic was cracked. He placed his hand on the glass in front of him, the other side so far away, yet so close. The bulletproof glass a barrier between two lives. Ryan's heart bounced within his chest, pounding against his ribs. His hands were sweaty, and he pushed his toes against the inside of his shoes, a sign of nervousness, a way to hide his fears and emotions. It was a habit he'd had since childhood, but one that had disappeared when he'd moved into the Cohens' house. Now as he sat waiting for his father, it returned.

Ryan looked through the glass and his stomach jumped. His toes pressed even harder against the inside of his shoes. The sight of his father was almost unbearable. He barely recognized him. His hair was long and the top was thin. The dirty blond had turned to brown and his eyes looked yellow, old, and sad. The thin skin around them was wrinkled, weathered. This was not the father Ryan remembered. The youthful man with a full head of dirty-blond hair, the young man who had shown him how to ride his bike. His father approached the other side of the glass. Miles away. Ryan's spine tingled and he instinctively reached for the leather band around his neck but it was gone. He remembered Marissa and Seth and the Cohens and the night he had tossed the leather band into the sea and watched it disappear below him. The night he had given up on becoming part of a family. And now as he sat here staring at his own father, who still wore the leather band around his own neck, he felt guilty and relieved all at once. He had a family now. His father was no longer his family. And as his father picked up the phone on the other side of the glass, Ryan hesitated, thought about running away, back to Chino or Newport, but he looked through the glass and when his father's eyes locked with his own he knew he had to stay.

Ryan picked up the phone on his side of the glass. His hand trembled as he brought the receiver up to his ear.

"Ryan," his father began in a husky, cigarette-laden voice.

"Hey," Ryan said, shaken by the sound of his father's voice in his ear. He pressed his toes against the inside of his shoes, hiding his emotions. *An Atwood man shows no fear.* He thought about Sandy waiting outside, and he wanted to get up and run.

"How's Trey?" his father asked, interrupting his thoughts.

"In jail."

His father's face fell, but not in a way of disappointment, in a sign that he knew it was coming. Almost like he expected it.

"And you got out?"

"Yeah," Ryan answered, avoiding the question. Just playing to his father's expectations.

"What kind of Atwood are you? Gettin' smart to the law. You supposed to be in jail. You always were the smart one, though, weren't you?"

"Yeah, I guess."

"Why you here? Your mom need money?"

Ryan shook his head no. He didn't even know where his mom was. He hadn't spoken to her since last fall. Since she had left him at the Cohens'. Ryan sat still. He didn't know how to bring it up, and then the words just burst out of his mouth.

"I'm going to be a father."

Ryan's father sat still for a moment, an angry look upon his face, then he jumped up from his seat and started shouting. "You knocked a girl up? What kind of —" Ryan sat back in his dusty chair, terrified. But then his father's face broke and he turned to another prisoner on his side of the impenetrable glass. "You hear that, guys? My son got some action. That's an Atwood for you. Knockin' em' up and leavin' 'em."

But Ryan couldn't listen to his father go on. "I didn't leave," he interrupted. "We're in Chino. The baby's on its way. And it might not be mine. But I need —"

"What the hell you stickin' around for, son?" his father asked, cutting him off. The words hanging heavy on Ryan's ears. And Ryan winced at the echo of the word "son." Because at that moment as he looked into his father's yellowed eyes, he realized he was his father's son.

He no longer needed to hear the truth. He already knew. His father was never a dad. His father never felt responsible, never felt that a child needed a chance, a dad, or a family. He never felt the way Ryan felt now toward Theresa and the baby.

Ryan slowly got up from his chair and let the phone drop from his hand. He stood still, wanting to run, but he couldn't turn around. Ryan watched the irate man bang on the thick glass, yelling into the phone, and he held strong as the guards surrounded his father and held him down. Ryan reached out and touched the glass, then turned around and walked out the door forever, without a single word.

Sandy tried to break the silence on the ride back to Chino, but Ryan quickly stopped him.

"Can we not talk about it?" he asked and placed his head on the cool glass of the window.

"Sure," Sandy said and turned up the radio. The soft sounds of Neil Young echoed through the car.

When they arrived back at Theresa's house, Ryan sat in the car as Sandy parked in the driveway and turned off the motor.

They sat silently for a moment, then Sandy spoke. "You know you don't have to do this."

Ryan shook his head yes. But in his heart he knew he had to, that if he didn't he would regret it forever. If he didn't, he would be just like his own father. He would be an abandoner. And as far as he knew there was only one Sandy Cohen. If he left the baby, who would be there to save it when it was older and found itself alone without a family? Who would rescue it? He had to do this. For himself. For his mom. For Theresa and Trey. He couldn't let another child grow up the same way he had. He couldn't repeat the cycle.

Ryan held out his hand to thank Sandy for the ride, but Sandy reached out for him and embraced him — hugging him like a son.

"He'll be back, you know," Ryan said as he peeled himself from Sandy's grip and got out of the car, shutting the car door behind him. The sound of Sandy's car revved, then faded away and Ryan knew he was in this forever.

Inside, Theresa sat watching TV, so he sat down next to her. Then he placed his hand upon hers, silently. She looked at him, and Ryan knew that she knew where he had gone. But neither said a word. He had one hope, a silent understanding as he looked into her eyes, a reason to make things work between them — he couldn't let this baby grow up without a father like he had.

Theresa looked at his hand, but he squeezed it harder. And he decided right then and there that he would make this work, that he would pretend if he had to. He would do it all for the baby.

6

Marissa lay next to Caleb's pool, soaking in the warmth of the California sun. Summer lay next to her in her red string bikini. Their two tiny bodies specks of sand on a mountain, lost in the monstrosity of the mansion that stood above them.

Summer turned over. "Flip."

Marissa followed suit, pulling her light brown hair off her face, twisting it until it stayed up on its own.

The two girls had been lying out for the last two hours, their skin slowly turning golden brown.

"I officially hate Cohen," Summer said, sitting up in her chair.

Marissa opened her eyes and looked at her friend. *What now?* she asked silently with her eyes.

"He's such an ass. Who calls you up to tell you that they miss you, and then proceeds to tell you about all the girls he's been meeting? And then has the nerve to ask if you've met anyone with the hopes that you've just been sitting around all summer pining away for him?"

Marissa just shrugged her shoulders. She'd spent the last couple days listening to Summer complain about Seth and the horrible phone call and she'd run out of things to say.

"Well, maybe you should stop waiting around," Marissa said, knowing that she was being harsh, but having no choice.

"I'm not waiting around," Summer said, on the defense. "What about that guy Zach? Totally flirting with me the other night."

"Summer, he poured you a margarita," Marissa answered. They had gone out a couple of nights ago, but the night had turned out to be a disaster and when Summer returned home that night Seth had called her.

"We made eye contact."

"Right," Marissa said, lying back down in her chair to continue soaking up the rays.

"I'm not waiting around," Summer began, but Marissa just nodded. "I've moved on. Cohen? Who's that?" Marissa lay still and said nothing. Summer leaned back and was about to lie down again when something caught her eye. The gorgeous gardener who Marissa had flirted with the other morning was standing nearby. Shirtless, his tan muscles glistening in the sun. "Coop, look," Summer whispered so he wouldn't hear her.

Marissa opened her eyes and turned her head to see what had caught Summer's eye. She recognized him immediately. The guy she had elusively undressed for behind the gauze of the curtains in her room. She smiled and he smiled back, then turned to continue pulling weeds from the flower beds.

"Cohen?" Summer started. "Totally erased by that guy's hotness. If he wasn't the gardener, I'd do him."

"Summer!" Marissa exclaimed with a giggle. "He's like —"

"Hot?"

"That. And standing right there." The girls looked at him again to make sure he hadn't heard their conversation. But the gardener just continued to work. His muscles tightening with each movement he made. Marissa couldn't take her eyes off him. She didn't care that he was the gardener. Her mind wandered. Fantasized. She wanted him to be her escape. To help her out of this hell that was Caleb's mansion. But the more she thought about him the more she knew it would never happen. Summer was right. He was the gardener. And she couldn't enter that territory. She could only look from a distance.

"I'm going in," Marissa started as she stood up from her chair. "It's too hot."

"'Kay," Summer said and followed her up the steps and into the house, both girls turning to take one last look at the shirtless gardener.

Inside the house, Marissa poured two glasses of water from the bottles of Fiji in the fridge.

Summer took a sip from her glass, then began, "So I think we should go to Nordlund's tonight. He and Saunders are throwing a party at his beach house. Maybe Zach will be there. And I can get him to pour me another margarita," she finished with a smile.

Marissa thought about the idea for a moment. The last time she went out with Summer in Newport she hadn't had that much fun, and she had remembered how much she hated the city, but she really didn't have any other plans.

"Fine," Marissa said. "On one condition. You come with me to the Plaza. I have nothing to wear."

"Fine, if you're forcing me. Then I guess I'll have to go shopping with you," Summer said sarcastically. And the girls laughed. With Summer around, Newport wasn't as bad as Marissa had painted it to be.

"I have to get a card from Caleb. Then we'll go."

Caleb's office smelled of new leather. Marissa knocked on the door and Caleb finally motioned for her to enter.

Summer followed her into the room. Caleb glared at them.

"Oh, sorry, this is Summer," Marissa said, noting Caleb's glare.

"I know who she is. Seth's old girl. You and Chino drove him out of here." Caleb returned to his papers. Summer was speechless. Marissa changed the subject.

"My mom said I could go shopping, but I needed to get the credit card from you."

"What am I, an ATM?"

"Nope. Just my evil stepfather," Marissa replied quickly with no remorse.

"I could have you grounded."

Summer gasped.

"And I could tell your precious Juju that you blackmailed me into living here."

"Fine. Here. Have fun." Caleb tossed his AmEx at her.

"Thanks." She smiled as she walked away with Summer following close behind.

"What's wrong with him?"

"I don't know. He's been acting weird lately. Kind of like my dad used to."

"What is he, like, stealing money from all of Newport? No offense to your dad."

Marissa nodded. *None taken.*

"I doubt it. But that would be funny if he lost all his money and my mom was poor again."

Summer laughed.

South Coast Plaza sat just east of the 405 freeway and claimed to be one of the largest shopping malls in Southern California. But the Plaza was not like any ordinary mall. This was Newport and, like all things Newport, it was full of money and prestige and every store imaginable straight off the streets of Paris and Milan. It was Rodeo Drive under a roof. A mall for the rich.

Marissa pulled her Jeep up to the front entrance and handed her keys to the valet. Summer got out of the passenger side and they entered the refined space. Inside, the mall was filled with teens their age, summer vacationers who had come down from up north, moms with babies, young couples in love. Marissa and Summer made their way through the crowds, browsing the windows of the stores until they came to Chanel.

Marissa sifted through the clothes until she found a skirt and top that screamed everything but Newport. It was bold and low cut and short.

She had to have it. No matter the price.

It was her next step toward declaring her independence from this city. To declaring that she was her own person.

She paid the cashier with Caleb's AmEx and the two girls set out to do more damage.

That night, as Marissa got ready she looked at the Pucci dress she had never worn and again at the Chanel outfit that she had bought that day. Neither were the Marissa anyone expected, but both were everything Marissa always wanted.

And so she finished her makeup and put on her new clothes. She felt beautiful and free and ready to go out. Even if she hated every moment of the party, at least she had an outfit that made her feel as though she had escaped to anywhere but here. Anywhere beyond the monotony of Newport.

For the first time since Ryan had left she felt whole, that she had escaped, her body cloaked in Chanel and her mind open to possibilities.

Downstairs, Marissa slipped out the front door

and into Summer's car waiting for her in the drive-way.

Nordlund's house was packed with people. Marissa and Summer entered side by side and took in their surroundings. There were kids out back doing keg-stands. A kitchen with a counter full of alcohol and mixers. Surfers taking hits off a bong in the corner and really skinny girls doing lines of coke off the dining room table.

"Welcome to the dark side," Marissa said sar-castically, not sure she really wanted to be here.

"Funny, Coop. Come on, we need drinks," Summer said, grabbing her friend's hand and lead-ing her through a group of girls dancing in their bikini tops and over to the kitchen where there was plenty of alcohol.

Summer picked up two cups and filled them with ice. "Vodka, rum, gin, whiskey. What do you feel like?" Summer asked as she sifted through the bottles.

"Um, something strong," Marissa replied as she gazed around the room. The last time she had been at a party like this was last September and she felt out of place. None of these people were her friends anymore. After her incident in Tijuana at the end of the previous summer, where she had overdosed on painkillers and tequila, most of her regular friends had disappeared. She had spent the majority of last year with Summer, Seth, and Ryan and sometimes Luke, but she hadn't really been a part of Newport.

The parties that kids threw at their parents' houses, the dances, the National Charity League events, once Ryan had entered her life she had slowly drifted away from those things. But now that Ryan was gone, and there was no guarantee that he would ever return, Marissa found herself back where she had started. Back in Newport. Back in the heart of the O.C. Unsure whether or not she really wanted to be there.

Summer handed Marissa her drink. A potent cup full of vodka and cranberry juice. Marissa sipped it and the coolness slipped down her throat. "Thanks," she said, the alcohol slowly removing her worries.

"Look who's here," Summer said softly as she sipped her own drink and motioned to the other side of the room.

Marissa looked over and saw Zach standing in the corner with a couple of his friends, chugging some beer.

"He's cute," Marissa said as she took another sip of her drink and looked around at the party.

"Real cute. I told you. Now come on, let's mingle." But before Summer could turn around and grab Marissa, Marissa dumped some more vodka in her drink. *This is going to be a long night*, she thought and followed Summer over to Zach and his friends.

"Hey, Zach," Summer started as she approached.

"Summer. You look" — and Zach looked her up and down — "beautiful, as always. And Marissa, you look lovely as well. I was just about to go to the kitchen. Can I get you ladies anything to drink?"

"I'm good," Summer said.

"A vodka with cranberry."

"Marissa," Summer exclaimed, looking at her friend's almost empty drink.

"What? I'm having fun like we used to," Marissa replied as she took the last sip of her drink, swirling it around in her mouth.

Summer just shrugged and looked over at Zach, who was pouring Marissa's next drink. Marissa sat down on one of the overstuffed couches and watched as Summer and Zach flirted with each other, winking and waving from opposite sides of the room. Marissa thought about Ryan, how she had done the same thing with him the first few times they met each other and she wondered what he was doing right now. If he and Theresa had gotten back together, if they were out having fun or watching movies or just hanging out and talking like she and Ryan used to do. And she wanted to call him and have him come over and rescue her from this party.

Zach returned with Marissa's drink and she tried to thank him, but he had already turned back to Summer. The two continued to flirt and laugh and talk and Marissa felt even more alone as she looked around the room, not recognizing anyone. Part of her felt happy that her efforts to escape Newport last year had worked, but she also felt down knowing that all her efforts had only led her back here a year later. But now she was no longer Marissa

Cooper, the queen of Newport, the girl with the perfect water-polo-playing boyfriend, the social chair, the head of National Charity League — she was Marissa Cooper and that was it. And being just Marissa Cooper was fine and easy when she had Ryan beside her, but now that she had no one, the thought of being Marissa Cooper scared her. She thought about taking the same route Summer was taking, throwing herself back into the social scene, but in her heart she knew that she couldn't do it. She knew that if she went back things would only get worse. Caleb's mansion would become her home, Caleb would become her father, and she would grow into the next Julie Cooper. But that was not what Marissa wanted. She downed her drink and walked back into the kitchen to get another while Summer and Zach continued to entrance each other.

"Marissa Cooper? No way!" Marissa turned around and saw her old friend Holly Fisher standing behind her. "That top is so not —" Marissa waited for Holly to finish. "So not you. But I like it. I thought you'd, like, disappeared. I mean I barely saw you at school last year and you never partied with us like you used to. I mean not after Tijua —" Marissa glared at her. Holly stopped herself from finishing her sentence and walked away. It had been a long time since Marissa had seen or spoken to Holly. Holly had been one of her friends when she was the queen of Newport, but once her father had gotten into his financial trouble and Holly had started hook-ing up with Luke, Marissa had decided that Holly was not only not her friend, but that she would never be her friend again.

Marissa finished pouring her drink and decided that she needed some fresh air. She took her cup, adding another splash of vodka, and headed out onto the back porch of Nordlund's house.

Out here the noise from inside was muffled by the crashing of the ocean waves. The tide was on its way in and Marissa watched the mist rise from each wave as it fell onto the warm sand. The alcohol continued to consume her. Her body tingled. Out here Marissa felt calm and alive, like she could face Newport on her own. She took another sip of her drink and sat on the back porch until her body was numb and her vision was blurred. If she was going to continue on in Newport, she'd have to do it drunk, or else she'd have to admit defeat and leave.

An hour later Marissa stumbled back into the house and found Summer kissing Zach.

"Let's go," Marissa slurred.

Summer pulled back from Zach and looked at her friend approaching. "Where were you? I was looking for you earlier."

"Outside. Can we go? I need to get out of here."

Summer looked back at Zach. "Don't you want to stay for just a bit longer?"

"Summer, I don't belong here." Marissa started walking for the door, but Summer didn't follow. "Never mind, I'll walk."

Again, Summer looked reluctantly at Zach, then back at Marissa. Marissa stood at the door alone, ready to leave.

"I'll come with you," Zach said. Then whispered to Summer, "You might need help carrying her inside."

"Thanks." Summer smiled as she followed Zach up to the door.

Marissa slurred the words "good night" to Summer and Zach and stumbled to the front door of Caleb's house as the two drove away. Under the light of the moon, Marissa found her key and slowly placed it in the lock, trying not to make too much noise. She didn't want to wake her mom or Caleb or her sister.

Once inside, Marissa tiptoed up the stairs and into her bedroom, where she drunkenly took off her new clothes and tossed them onto the floor. As she stood in her bra and panties she looked at the photo of her and Ryan next to the bed and thought about how much she missed him. How the last time she had become this depressed and turned to alcohol for escape he had saved her. But now as she stood here alone in her room in this strange house, there was no one to save her. She walked out onto the balcony of her room. The cool night's breeze danced upon her exposed skin, and she let the moon's glow illuminate her for all of Newport to see. Deep down she knew that no one was looking. That even now as she stood here in her underwear for all the world to see, no one cared.

So she went back inside and put on a T-shirt and a pair of pajama pants and grabbed a bottle from her stash. She crept out of her room, down through the house, and out into the backyard. Past the patio and the pool and the pool house and out into the grass and the trees and the flowers until she sat at the edge of the yard. At the edge of Newport. Drinking straight from the bottle. Ready to leap. Ready to say good-bye to it all.

And she continued to drink until the alcohol overtook her and she passed out in the damp, dark grass.

When she awoke Marissa found herself not in the dew of the morning grass, but in the comfort of a bed. A small bed she had never seen before. A sense of fear washed over her. Where was she? What had happened? The last thing she remembered was sitting at the edge of Caleb's yard, drinking. What had she done?

She sat up quickly, but the alcohol still rang through her head and she quickly lay back down. She was alive at least. A strong smell of dryer sheets sprang into her senses. Then Marissa heard a noise. Someone was coming. She thought about hiding or running, but couldn't. She didn't know where she was. Frightened, she pulled the sheets up over her head as the sound got closer.

Someone had entered the room. Maybe Summer had taken her back to Nordlund's or Zach's. Slowly she pulled back a corner of the sheet and peeked out the side. And the sight made her gasp for air and her heart leap.

It was the gardener she had been flirting with for the last two weeks.

Marissa pulled back the rest of the sheets and slowly sat up in bed. The hot gardener had brought her back to his place. But still she had no clue how or why or when.

"You're . . . How did I?" she started.

"Sorry, I meant to be here when you woke up. I went to get you some water. Here." He handed her a glass of cool water. Marissa sipped it down quickly, her body dehydrated.

"Did I call you?" Marissa asked, still utterly confused. Why was he being so nice to her?

"I went to work early. Almost ran you over with the lawn mower. You were passed out in the yard. And I figured. Well, I knew. If my parents found me passed out drunk in my yard I wouldn't see the light of day for months."

"I can take care of myself," Marissa said defensively, snapping at him. What did a gardener know?

"You were shivering." He reached out and placed a hand on her shoulder. She tried to move away. "Much warmer now."

Again she tried to pull away, but chills ran up her spine. Something about his touch was soothing. Different. Comforting.

Marissa smiled at him. The hot gardener had turned into more than just a gardener. More than just a pretty guy Marissa could stare at and imagine escaping with . . . then she realized why: He'd saved her.

"I'm DJ," he said.

"Marissa."

"I know."

"You do?" she asked.

He nodded. "You and your friend are always talking. I can hear you two. I'm just a pretty yard boy."

"Oh. Thank you?" she said. Then she placed her hand on his shoulder. The chills returned. Only this time she could see them run through DJ as well.

And he reached out and grabbed her face and kissed her forehead, in a friendly, comforting gesture. "You're welcome." He got up to leave.

But Marissa couldn't let him pull away. There was something about him that made her whole body tingle, that made it feel better than any alcohol she'd ever had, and she took it as a sign. A sign that DJ was all things to come. All things that weren't Newport. Her escape. Her ticket out. Even if it were only for a moment.

Without thinking, she pulled him closer and wrapped her arms around him, then she kissed him on the lips and their tongues flitted against each other. Not knowing what had come over her, just letting things happen.

"Is this okay?" she asked, more for herself than anyone else. DJ nodded yes and they continued to kiss.

But as her hands started to wander, he pulled back. "Are you sure? This is not just . . . you know."

"I know. I don't care," Marissa replied with a smile.

And his hands began to wander along her body. Caressing her. She didn't stop him. At that moment she didn't care who he was, the gardener or otherwise. Right now he was an escape.

They both lay in the bed kissing, touching. Holding each other. A magnetic force drawing them closer and closer with each kiss. With each touch. And Marissa knew what was about to happen and she let herself drift closer and closer to sex with DJ the gardener. Because she knew, she had finally found someone to rescue her. To take her out of Newport. And as they moved closer, Marissa thought about Ryan, how they had shared so much, but never made love. And slowly, she let Ryan's memory become replaced with this new face in front of her. DJ. The gardener. Her savior.

And when they lay exhausted, Marissa turned to DJ and smiled and said, "Thank you." A thank-you for rescuing her from her yard, from Newport, from jumping over the cliff.

He kissed her forehead and smiled back and then they stood up and got dressed. It was seven in the morning and they were both expected back at the Nichol mansion, but for vastly different reasons.

The ride back to the mansion was quiet. Marissa panicked a bit. Was this a one-night stand? She looked at DJ and she knew in her heart that this was something more. The attraction between them was loud. They had shared themselves with each other and there was no turning back.

DJ continued to speed toward Caleb's.

"Did I make you late?" she asked, finally breaking the awkward silence.

DJ nodded yes. "I don't care. It was worth it no matter how much Caleb Nichol is going to yell at me."

"Yeah." Marissa smiled, thinking about what Caleb would say to her if he caught her sneaking back into the house. "He's kind of a —"

"Rich jerk?" DJ asked.

Marissa laughed, then nodded yes.

"No offense, but the guy's an arrogant bastard."

"I know."

"Well, at least we've got something in common. That's a start, right?"

Marissa smiled and took solace in the fact that she had finally found someone else besides her father who found Caleb Nichol as repulsive as she did.

DJ pulled up to the end of the hill and stopped the car.

"Um, we probably shouldn't —"

"Oh, right," Marissa said as she unbuckled her seat belt. "I can walk the rest."

"Will I see you?" he asked. She shrugged her shoulders. She didn't know. What was she doing? Becoming an adult? Or a girlfriend?

But DJ just nodded and sped away. Marissa walked through the yard and up to the pool and into the house. How could she know what this was?

85

She'd never felt such an immediate attraction in her life, besides Ryan. Was DJ replacing Ryan?

She lay down on her bed and swallowed several aspirin. Then she pulled up the sheets and tried to fall asleep. But the picture of Ryan kept her awake. Finally she turned the picture over and put it face-down on the nightstand.

She had a new escape. A new fate. A secret life in the O.C.

7

The Portland air blew crisp and clean against the sail of the boat. Seth was out in the water teaching another lesson.

"Come about," Seth yelled into the breeze as the little boy steered and the sail flew from one side of the boat to the other. The boat steadied and the sail luffed for a minute then filled with air and became tight in the wind. Their speed picked up again. "Good job." Seth held up his hand and the boy gave him a high five.

At the end of the hour, Seth and the young boy sailed back into the harbor and docked the boat.

"You're looking really good out there. Same time tomorrow?" Seth asked. But the little boy just nodded. He never said much. "Okay, see you then."

As the boy walked off, Seth thought about teaching sailing lessons last summer in Newport. The little boy from today reminded him of Chester. Another quiet little kid who was a quick learner but never said much.

And Seth remembered the first time he and

Ryan had gone sailing. Ryan had been so scared of the water and Seth had been scared of Ryan, and afraid that Ryan would hate him, too, just like all the other kids in Newport. But Ryan had become his friend. And when he'd gotten in a fight with Luke and his crew, Ryan had come to his rescue.

And he thought how ironic that Luke was the one who had come to his rescue when Ryan had left. *Things change over just a year*, Seth thought as he folded up the sail for the evening.

"Hey, Cohen." Luke came bounding down the steps to the docks. "Dude, I just met two of the hottest girls ever."

Seth finished tying the folded sail to the boat, then looked up at Luke and beyond him at the top of the docks where two fairly gorgeous girls stood. The girls waved and Seth waved back.

"Is that them?" Seth asked.

Luke turned around and looked at the two girls. "Yeah. They're hot, right?"

Seth looked at them again. "I'm not arguing."

"You're coming with us."

"Where?"

"Out. I don't know. Wherever the night leads us. Two hot girls. You and me. There are endless possibilities."

"I am not having an orgy with you."

"Dude, gross. Wasn't thinking that way."

"Fine. But I can't stay out all night."

"Fine. Two A.M., then."

"Luke."

"That's when the bars close back home."

"Luke, you never went to bars back home."

"They don't know that."

Seth sighed. "I'm leaving early. I have to wake up at six-thirty to meet Cali. We're leaving for Astoria tomorrow."

"Fine." Luke walked off and back up the dock to meet the girls.

"Fine."

Seth had learned not to argue with Luke over these things. If Luke wanted to go out all night, Seth just went along. And as soon as Luke became occupied with a girl or drinking beer, Seth was free to sneak off and do what he pleased. Most of the time he stayed and hung out with Luke and their new friends, but there were times, like tonight, when he had things to do in the early morning.

Seth put the last tie on the boat and went up to join Luke and the girls.

"Cohen," Luke said as Seth approached. "This is Amanda." She reached out her hand and Seth shook it. "And this," Luke started, giving Seth the eye—the eye that said *this girl is for you.* "This is Jane."

"Nice to meet you," Seth replied as he shook her hand. Her skin soft against his. Her eyes held him, checking him out. Seth felt her looking at him, and his cheeks rushed with blood. Blushing.

"You too," Jane replied, smiling.

Seth finally dropped her hand.

"All right," Luke said as he headed to his truck. "What are we going to do?"

The girls followed close behind with Seth bringing up the rear. Luke held the door open and the girls climbed into the backseat of the truck.

"Let's go somewhere mellow," Amanda said as Luke started the engine.

"We have to give lessons early tomorrow morning," Jane chimed in. "I can't stay out late."

Seth smiled. He kind of liked this girl. She worked. Like him. And she was responsible. *This could be good*, he thought. Something to get his mind off Summer. Something to make him forget the horrible phone call they'd had. Yes, he thought, she could be the ace bandage over the knee that masked the pain, but didn't actually heal it. She was cute and after the phone call he didn't expect to see Summer anytime soon. He wondered if Jane liked comic books and Death Cab, and if she was smart.

"We should go to our place," Seth suggested, hoping Luke would go for it and not get scared about his dad and Gus. Since Seth had lived at the Wards' Luke hadn't brought a single girl home. Seth wondered if he would ever get over his embarrassment.

"Cohen, we can't," Luke said with a stern look toward Seth.

"Oh, come on," Amanda begged in a sweet voice from behind Luke's seat. "Don't you live on the water? We could start a bonfire."

"Yeah. Roast marshmallows. Make s'mores. It's like heaven, Luke. Hot, gooey marshmallow and chocolate. What could be bad about that?" Luke glared at him. *What about my dad?* "Except the cleanup. The sticky feel on your fingers. But that's nothing."

"Come on," Jane said.

"You heard the ladies," Seth said.

"Fine, but we'll hang out outside in the back. We're not going inside."

"We know about your dad."

"How?"

"Petey. And word travels fast. Don't worry about it, though. We're cool with it."

"See, I told you Portland was much more understanding than Newport," Seth added.

"To my house it is." Luke smiled.

Seth smiled back. He liked that people were so understanding here. That for once in his life if he said everything was going to be okay, things usually ended up okay.

The bonfire blazed hot and orange in the backyard. All four sat around the fire roasting marshmallows, licking the white stickiness from the tips of their fingers.

"So you sailed here?" Jane asked Seth.

"If Greyhound has boats now," Luke chimed in from the other side of the fire, his face distorted by the heat.

Jane looked at Seth.

"Slight glitch in the details. Either way, I made it here alone."

"Wow," Amanda said, her mouth open. "That's pretty cool."

Seth smiled thanks, then shoved a graham cracker into his mouth.

"I always wanted to do the Jack Kerouac thing," Jane said.

"Me too," Seth said through a mouthful of food.

Luke stabbed his marshmallow into the open fire, then smiled at Amanda.

"What's that?" Luke asked.

"The book. *On the Road*," Jane responded as Amanda just shrugged her shoulders.

"Oh," Luke said as he pulled his crispy marshmallow out of the fire and placed it between two crackers and a piece of chocolate. Amanda looked at Luke then at his s'mores. He handed it to her and the two of them started talking, leaving Seth and Jane alone.

"So. Life on the open road, huh? Never knowing where you could end up next. Meeting all those different people. Must have been fun," Jane said to Seth as she inched a bit closer to him.

"Yeah," he said. "No."

Jane looked at him inquisitively. Her perfect image of the traveling Seth Cohen shattered.

"You know who rides those buses?"

Jane shook her head no.

"No one you'd like to know."

"But it sounds so . . . You didn't meet anyone?"

Seth was about to say no, when he remembered Cali. How they had met on the bus and how he had to get up in a few hours to meet her and he hadn't even packed.

"I mean, I met people. I actually met this really great girl," Seth said as he thought about Cali.

"Oh," Jane said, inching away from him.

"No. It's not like that. She's older. We're really good friends now. She's kind of like the older sister I never had."

"I'm an only child," Jane answered.

"Me too. Well, I had a brother —"

"I'm sorry." Jane placed her hand on Seth's arm. A gesture of comfort.

"No. See he was from Chino." Jane looked at him, clueless. "Right. Chino's sort of like the ghetto. Anyways, my dad's a public defender. Or he was. And he was defending Ryan and then Ryan's mom left him and he had nowhere to go, so my parents kind of took him in. Adopted him. And then we were brothers. Actually, better friends," Seth started.

"Where is he now?" Jane asked.

Seth took a breath, trying to control his anger. "He went back to Chino. Kind of just left me in the dark."

"I'm sorry," Jane said, now placing her hand on top of Seth's.

"No, it's fine," Seth said, pulling his hand away. "I'm here now. And I'm happy. Which reminds me. I'm sailing to Astoria tomorrow with Cali." Seth stood up from the ground. "I've got to go pack." Luke and Amanda broke off their conversation and looked over at Seth.

"Jane, it was really nice to meet you." Seth held out his hand and the two shook. "I'm sure I'll see you around."

"Yeah," Jane answered. "We should get going, too. Amanda, are you ready?"

Luke stood up and gave Amanda his hand to help her, too.

"Don't leave because of me," Seth said. "You guys stay. Luke will keep you company."

Seth walked off without a second glance back. He could feel Jane staring and he felt bad for leaving so abruptly, but he had things to do.

Upstairs, Seth packed his bag for the trip with Cali. Sweatshirts, shorts, a few T-shirts, and his sketchbook. He had begun drawing this summer. It had started on the bus as a way to keep himself occupied and avoid eye contact with any of the other passengers, but the more he drew and refined his sketches, the better his ideas became. Right now he was working on a series of sketches that resembled himself and his friends. They were comic versions of themselves and each one of them had superpowers, which he was still working out. The details weren't in place, but it felt like he had a good beginning, a new direction for his life. Something more than sailing. Something more than a life in Newport.

Seth put the sketchbook in the bag with all his other things and zipped it up. There was a knock on the door.

"Dude, I can't believe you bailed so early. Those girls were so into us."

"Yeah," Seth said as he sat on the edge of his bed. So close to sleep yet so far away.

"So, you and Jane? Hey? You guys have a lot in common."

"As friends. Friends always have a lot in common."

"But doesn't that make it better?"

"I already got one Seth Cohen in my life. I don't need another. I'm hard enough to keep up with as it is."

"That's true," Luke said as he flopped down onto Seth's bed. "But what about Amanda? She's pretty hot, yeah?"

"Yeah."

"I think I'm going to go for it."

"And I think you should. But for now, I really need to get some sleep."

"Oh. Right. Sorry. Astoria with Cali. Hey, what about the two of you? You ever think of, you know?"

"No. She's like a sister. I'd go for Jane before Cali and I ever tried anything."

"Just checking. See you in a few days."

"See you," Seth said as he watched Luke shut the door behind himself.

As Seth lay in bed, waiting for sleep to overcome him, he thought about this night and about the conversation he and Luke just had. Why had he been so reluctant to go after Jane? She was cute. They had a lot in common. And she was fun. She was the girl version of Seth Cohen. What more could he ask for?

The moon outside drifted through the window.

And then it hit him. He had already dated the girl version of himself: Anna Stern. And while everything seemed perfect on paper between them, they had realized that they were much better as friends. That they were so similar that they loved each other only as friends. And that's when he had gone to Summer.

And that's when it hit him. Why he couldn't go after Jane.

If he was going to hook up with anyone and risk screwing up everything with Summer, he'd have to make sure he was really ready. That he was not just chasing after another Anna.

The sun had just barely risen over the horizon as Seth and Cali threw their bags into the boat and prepared to set sail for the day.

Cali had spent the last few weeks since she'd arrived in Portland working for a family as a sort of nanny, maid, and cook all rolled into one. Sometimes she spent her days chasing the little three-year-old around and playing with him, or sometimes she cooked dinner and cleaned the house. Her life was never dull. And the latest task she'd been given was to sail the Reeds' boat to Astoria where they had a summer place so that they could take it out for day sails.

"Never understood why they would have a bedroom down here if they were never going to take it anywhere overnight," Cali said, smiling as she came up from belowdeck.

"It's like having earthquake insurance in Iowa. What's the point?" Seth laughed.

"My point exactly," Cali said as she passed by Seth and started untying the sails.

Seth threw his bag belowdeck then began to help Cali get the boat.

And as they sailed away from the dock, Seth stood in the bow, letting the wind blow through his hair, and he breathed in the crisp, clean air of Portland and thought this must be what it's like to feel at home. To feel like everything around you is there for you. That you are not an outsider. That the world you live in is your home.

"Hey, Leo, you want to come back here and help me?" Cali screamed from the stern as she tried to man the rudder and the mainsail.

"Yes, my dear Rose," Seth said as he maneuvered his way to the back of the boat and grabbed the ropes controlling the sail. "Your Jack is here. Come with me to the other side. Where the people are real."

Cali laughed. "Okay, James Cameron. This is not the *Titanic*. You got that sail?"

Seth smiled as he held up the ropes. The wind blowing through his hair. He was glad that he had met Cali on the bus. That they had remained friends and that they were spending the next two days together. When he was with her, he felt like he was Sal Paradise. That she was Dean Moriarty. And when she was in charge he never knew what could happen.

As the sun set and the wind died down, Seth sat drawing in his sketchbook. His pencil moving quickly over the white of the paper, his thoughts came to life. His dreams.

"Is that her?" Cali asked, startling him.

He nodded yes and she sat down next to him. The boat drifted on autopilot. The light wind pushed them along.

"She's beautiful."

Seth smiled. She was beautiful. Summer had always been beautiful and now as he sat here drawing her, she seemed so far away. "Thanks," he said as he continued to sketch.

"Did she ever write you back?" Cali asked.

Seth had told Cali the back story of him and Summer, and he had asked her advice on every letter he'd written her since he'd been in Portland. He shook his head no. But what he didn't tell Cali was that he'd never sent the letters.

"She doesn't know what she's missing."

"Pretty sure she does," Seth said, remembering their phone call. "I called her the other day. It didn't go that well."

"I'm sure it wasn't as bad as you think. What'd she say?"

"That she never wanted to hear my Cohen voice again."

Cali cringed. She shouldn't have asked. "Well, you're here now. Let's enjoy it."

That night as they anchored about five hours from Astoria, Seth and Cali lay on deck sipping some whiskey they had found in one of the cabinets in the bedroom below.

"This kind of tastes like —" Seth began.

"Piss," Cali finished.

"Rubbing alcohol. Or piss." Seth took another sip, then swallowed. "I'd say piss."

Cali took the bottle from Seth and sat up to take another sip. "Rubbing alcohol. Definitely."

They both laughed. Seth liked hanging around Cali. He never felt like he had to pretend about anything with her.

Cali passed the bottle back, and Seth poured a little in his mouth as he looked up at the bright sky above him. The stars twinkled white and gold against the darkness. In Newport, even though they were forty-five miles south of Los Angeles, the lights of the cities shone too bright and muted the beauty of the night sky. But up here, where most of the land was covered by forest preserves or mountains, Seth could see every star in the sky.

"There's Cepheus," Cali said, pointing out a constellation in the night. "King of the sky."

"Looks more like a house to me," Seth replied as he looked up at the polka-dotted darkness. The five points of the constellation shining bright in the night, in the shape of a home.

"You ever think you'll go back?" Cali asked.

Seth was quiet for a moment. Except for his parents, there was really nothing for him to go home to. He and Summer were on the outs. Ryan had left. Marissa was probably on Summer's side and other than that, there was no one in Newport that he had grown close to over the past year. Or at all. The only one he had left behind was Captain Oats, and though he was sure that he'd understand, he doubted the companionship of the plastic horse. "I don't think so," he finally replied.

"Me neither," Cali said.

"To Newport?" Seth asked.

"No," Cali laughed as she swallowed another sip of whiskey. "Back home."

"Where is that? I don't think you ever told me. Miss Mysterious."

"What's home anyways?" Cali asked as she stood up at the edge of the boat, the railing tight against her legs. "This is home," she screamed as she held out her arms and reached up to the sky and the open water below them and the hills beyond them. "Here," she said. And reached out her hand for Seth. He grabbed it and the two stood at the edge of the boat together. Both of their arms outstretched. To the sky. To the world. To home.

"It's you and me," she whispered. "It's us. Our friends. The people we meet. The places we've been. The company we've kept. It's everything and nothing. Everywhere and nowhere. It's just us being."

Seth nodded and reached for the bottle again, but Cali held it away. "You don't need that."

"I don't?" Seth asked.

Cali shook her head no, then disappeared be-lowdeck, leaving Seth all alone. A slight buzz ran through his body, but he wasn't drunk, just happy. Just happy to be here. With Cali. With Luke. With his two dads. Everything that wasn't Newport.

Even the thought of Summer and their horrible phone call was slowly dripping from his mind. He had Cali. The world. The sky.

Seth smiled and let the buzz carry him.

"You need this," Cali exclaimed as she came up from belowdeck holding a Ziploc bag full of things.

Seth walked over and sat next to her on the bench toward the back of the boat. The light of the moon danced above them, and the contents of the bag became clear. Cali had a bag full of mari-juana. And a small pipe.

Seth looked at it strangely. He'd seen people do pot at parties, but it wasn't something any of his friends had ever done and he'd never been tempted to try it.

But now as he sat here with Cali, somehow it had a new appeal. It represented an experience to him. A way to make this his home. A way to bring Cali into his home.

Cali pulled out the pipe and placed bits of the weed into the end. Then she lit the lighter and inhaled. The potent smoke filled her mouth and her lungs, and when she exhaled, the smoke blew past Seth's face.

She handed the pipe to Seth and he held it awkwardly in his hand. His inexperience showed.

Cali placed her hand on top of his and showed him how to hold the pipe, where to place his mouth. Then she lit the end for him. And he inhaled. The smoke filled his lungs and he felt the experience come over him. He felt different. Elated.

Until the smoke started to burn and he started coughing.

Cali hit him on the back and gave him some water to sip.

"Don't worry," she said. "You'll get used to it."

Then she took the pipe back from him and inhaled. Blowing smoke rings into the Oregon sky. Clouding out the stars momentarily.

And Seth continued to smoke until the two of them were high. Until the world felt like theirs. That they could control everything.

8

Ryan had spent the last week pretending. Pretending that everything was going to be just fine. That he knew how to be a father, that he and Theresa would be fine, but in his heart he knew this would never last. No one could pretend forever. At some point the facade they built up around themselves would have to come crashing down.

Each day was a challenge, another day on stage. And Ryan was worn out. Sundays were always the hardest days, the saddest.

Ryan and Theresa sat on the couch watching TV. Ryan flipped to a rerun of *The Valley*.

"Turn it," Theresa demanded. He didn't want to argue, so he flipped the channel. A baseball game appeared on screen. Ryan paused for just a second. "Ugh," Theresa said, disgusted.

"Sorry," Ryan said, quickly changing the channel again. But there was nothing on. There rarely ever was on a Sunday.

He handed Theresa the remote. He didn't want

to be responsible anymore. It wasn't his fault there was nothing on TV.

She took the remote and began to rapidly flip through the channels so that each commercial or program blurred into the next. The effect was dizzying.

"Stop," Ryan said aloud, his voice harsher than he wanted.

"No," Theresa snapped. "My TV."

"Fine," Ryan said, standing up.

"Where are you going?"

"Out. I don't know."

"No you're not," Theresa replied. "You promised you'd stay with me today." She flipped through the channels even faster. Her anger cycling and blurring on the screen.

"For what?"

"For what? My mom's gone all day. What if something happens? To me. The baby?"

"What are you talking about? Nothing's going to happen."

"What if I fell down the stairs?"

"This is a one-story house. What stairs?"

"What are we fighting about?"

"I don't know. The TV?" Ryan asked.

"There's nothing on."

"Right. My point exactly."

Theresa tossed the remote at him, then stormed off to her room. "Take your point."

Ryan stood in the center of the room. The words of a televangelist echoed from the TV as a man proclaimed that God worked in mysterious ways. That everything always worked out. That there was a reason for everything. That you just had to have faith. Ryan wanted to throw the remote at the TV.

How did some man on the TV know what was going on with him? In his head? His thoughts? Ryan hit the power button. The man's voice cut off with just one touch.

Now Ryan could hear Theresa crying in her room. His heart sank. He felt guilty. What had they really been fighting about in the first place? Nothing. And he had caused a huge scene. But she had fought back. Was this how things were going to be with them forever? Would they keep on trying to pretend that everything was fine? That they could make it as parents? What about when the baby actually arrived, what if it wasn't his, would they pretend then? Would he be the father no matter what? He'd accepted responsibility regardless but what would they say to the child? Would they have to live a lie forever? Would they have to pretend? And then when they couldn't pretend any longer would they fight about nothing?

Ryan shuddered at the thought.

Theresa's cries became louder. More audible.

Ryan walked to Theresa's room and knocked on the door. She didn't answer. He let himself in, shutting the door behind him.

Theresa was folded up on her bed, her face buried in her pillow. Ryan sat next to her and stroked her long hair.

Theresa continued to sob.

"I'm sorry," Ryan said softly.

The sobbing slowed, followed by deep breaths.

Then Theresa turned over and faced him. "It wasn't the TV, was it?" she asked.

Ryan shook his head no. Theresa nodded.

"So then, what?" she asked.

Ryan sat for a moment and thought about his answer. Could they pretend forever? And if so, was he ready to take on that burden? But Ryan knew they couldn't keep on like this.

"Maybe we stop lying. To each other."

"To ourselves," Theresa added.

"When things aren't good we —" But Ryan couldn't finish. The doorbell rang and interrupted his sentence. "I should get that."

Ryan got up from the bed. "I'll be right back," he added. Theresa sat up, drying the tears from her cheeks.

As he walked he thought about what he would say to Theresa. He was going to tell her that they needed to start being honest with each other. That they didn't need to pretend that everything was going to be fine. If they were scared they needed to say so. If they were mad, they needed to yell. They couldn't keep living this lie. They couldn't keep pretending to be adults.

He opened the door expecting to find someone trying to sell him something but there was no one there to sell him anything, no kid with a box of M&M's, no man selling cleaning products, just a woman with a bag full of gifts. It was Kirsten.

Ryan took a step back. She was the last person he expected to see in Chino. Especially today.

Kirsten reached out and embraced him without saying a word. Her soft arms around him made him feel calm and comforted. It felt good to have an adult around. A mother who wasn't Theresa's. His own mother.

When they let go of each other, Ryan motioned for her to come inside.

"I can't stay long," she started. "I was just out shopping. Trying to get away from the house. They're remodeling, you know." Ryan shook his head. He didn't know. "Anyway, I saw these things and I thought you might need them." Kirsten held up the bag. It was filled to the brim with clothes and accessories and diapers and bottles. Everything a new baby would need. "And I thought you'd been working hard. And I didn't have any of my sons around. And no one was eating all the bagels and I didn't have to go grocery shopping all the time now and I had some extra time and I —"

"Thank you," Ryan said, cutting off Kirsten's rambling speech. He sensed her uneasiness and he knew. Sandy had been right. Things with Kirsten and Seth hadn't been going so well, and he sensed that she was trying to make up for it with him. That she didn't want him to run away as well. "This is really nice of you."

"You didn't have to do that," Theresa said, appearing from the bedroom behind Kirsten, her eyes a little less swollen now.

Kirsten turned around and ran to Theresa and hugged her, too.

"Look at you," Kirsten said as she pulled away from Theresa and looked at her swollen belly. "You look so —"

"Pregnant," Theresa finished.

"Beautiful," Kirsten added as she touched Theresa's belly.

"Thanks," Theresa said, a bit embarrassed.

Ryan went into the kitchen and came back with three glasses of water and set them at the dining room table, trying to be the good host.

The three sat around and talked as Theresa rifled through all the clothes and gifts Kirsten had brought over.

"So, how are you two?" she asked.

Ryan and Theresa looked at each other. Should they tell the truth? Or keep on pretending? Ryan cautioned Theresa with his eyes. Who would say the first word? Who would lie?

"We're great," he finally blurted out. Now he could never finish his speech to Theresa.

Kirsten looked at Theresa, but Theresa did not let on. "Yeah, everything's good. Ryan's been taking me to all my appointments."

"No mood swings, madness? Morning sickness?" Kirsten asked.

"Nope," Theresa replied.

"'Cause I remember when I was pregnant with Seth, Sandy hated me. I was a wreck. I was moody. I was mean. I don't know how I put up with myself."

"No, Theresa's been great," Ryan added, knowing where Kirsten was going with her story. Knowing that Kirsten knew things were not perfect between him and Theresa. But now that he'd started the lie, that he had put on the facade in front of someone other than Theresa, he could never go back. People expected things now.

"Good." Kirsten looked at her watch and smiled at the both of them. "I should go, Sandy'll be back from the golf course soon, and I'm sure he's probably expecting some sort of takeout."

Ryan got up and walked Kirsten to the door. Theresa sat in her chair, too tired to move.

"Take care," Kirsten said from the door back to Theresa.

"Thank you for everything."

"Anytime." Kirsten smiled.

"Thank you. Really," Ryan said as he gave Kirsten a hug good-bye. Then he whispered in her ear, "He'll come home, you know." Kirsten squeezed him a little harder. A thanks.

And he watched as Kirsten drove away and he thought about Sandy and how the two of them were pretending. How they were doing anything they could to keep their minds off Seth, to forget that they were without their son, without their boys. And then Ryan thought about it some more and he wondered, *Is that how adults made it through this world? Is that why they always seemed to know everything? Were they just pretending?* And if so, did that mean he and Theresa were ready for this baby? Was learning to pretend a part of growing up, a part of becoming an adult, a mother, a father?

Ryan looked at Theresa and she forced a smile. The charade was on. They'd lied to someone besides themselves. They were adults. Pretending.

The next morning, Ryan awoke to find that Theresa had made him breakfast. He got up from the couch and folded his blankets, then made his way into the kitchen. In front of him sat a plate full of eggs and bacon and toast and orange juice.

"This looks good," Ryan said as he sat down and picked up his fork to start eating.

"You're welcome," Theresa said with a sweet smile, then sat down across from him and watched him eat his entire breakfast.

"Not hungry?" he asked.

"I ate earlier. You were still asleep."

"Oh," Ryan responded, then finished the eggs on his plate and wiped them up with a piece of toast.

"So, I was thinking," Theresa began, "that I could start giving you rides to and from work. It's so hot out there, and you always come home so exhausted I just thought it might be nice for a change."

Ryan dropped his fork. Surprised. What had gotten into her? Did she expect something from him now? "Sure," he finally said. "You don't have to, though. My bike is fine."

"I want to."

* * *

The ride to work was awkward. Neither one of them said a word. And when Theresa pulled up in front of the site where Ryan was working, she handed him a brown paper bag.

"What's this?" Ryan asked.

"Lunch."

Ryan smiled, then went to get out of the car, but stopped himself. As long as they were pretending, he might as well go all the way, so he leaned over and tried to kiss her on the lips.

But Theresa pushed him away. "I — I thought . . ." he stuttered, but then stopped himself. "Never mind." And he leaped out of the car and didn't look back as Theresa's car drove out of sight.

Confusion overwhelmed Ryan for the rest of the day, affecting his ability to work. He was too distracted. What kind of game was Theresa playing?

That night Ryan got home well after the streetlights had come on and the sun had set. Theresa had never shown up to drive him home. The walk back had taken him an hour and now, more than ever, he was utterly confused. Was she only pretending for the morning? Was this a new form of morning sickness? But Ryan was tired of thinking, tired of trying to decipher this charade, and as he stood outside the house he found that he couldn't enter.

He took a deep breath.

Tonight he couldn't pretend.

Tonight, he needed an escape.

He turned away and started walking through the neighborhood. He hadn't walked through here since he'd moved back in with Theresa. Memories of his childhood began to flood his mind. Each house had a story. A specific memory. The time he and Theresa had t.p.'d old man Rangely's backyard. The whole two tiny trees he had just planted. The fun they had. And now as Ryan passed Mr. Rangely's he saw that the two trees now stood tall, shading the house.

Ryan continued to walk.

Mr. Ramirez was outside with his two daughters, happier than ever. Helping them put away their toys for the night.

Ryan smiled and waved, then took a few steps and stood under the streetlight and watched as it flickered on and off. The light danced upon his head, and he waved his hand. His shadow played tricks on the sidewalk, a strobe-light effect.

He was easily amused tonight.

He'd never realized how much charm, how much history his old neighborhood had. How much he had forgotten in just the year that he had spent in Newport. That he had spent trying to become a part of a new family.

How much Chino was still a part of him.

And Ryan continued to walk until he came to his old house.

The last time Ryan had been to this house he had returned to find it completely empty. His mom had abandoned him and left a note, saying good-bye, saying that she couldn't do it anymore. That she had given up on being a mother.

Ryan looked at the door now. It was closed and painted a new color and the lock looked like it worked.

He looked down at the gravel driveway and re-membered when Sandy had stood behind him watching. Waiting. As Ryan took the longest walk home ever, and he remembered how Sandy had waited with him the whole time. How Sandy had taken him back to Newport and brought him in, and he started to miss his home. His family. Seth and Kirsten and Sandy. And he wondered what they were all doing now. If they were as miserable as he was.

Ryan sat down on the sidewalk and let his emo-tions sift through his body. He was tired from a long day in the sun, and he was tired of pretending, or pretending not to pretend, or whatever it was that he and Theresa were doing. And he worried about becoming a father. And that he wasn't saying the right things to Theresa, and that this thing between them might never work. But worse than that he worried that he was losing his oldest friend.

Ryan remembered when Theresa used to be his comfort. When this house used to be full of shouts of anger and drunkenness, and he would hide out at Theresa's and spend the night and they would stay up until the early morning just talking and he missed those times. And he wondered why Theresa's pregnancy had to end their friendship. Why the one thing that brought him here by her side was the one thing that was driving them apart?

Ryan looked to the house for answers. For some key in the past that would help now or in the future. That would tell him that everything would be all right. That he could stop worrying.

He breathed in the cool, dusty air of Chino, his life breath, his roots, and spit it out with disgust. Was this all there was? An empty house on a darkened street.

But then as he turned to walk away he saw just inside the windows into the kitchen — a young family enjoying dinner together. Ryan paused. A shiver ran down his spine. Perhaps this was all he needed. A sign. A key from the past to open the future.

All his past was erased by the image of the family enjoying their dinner. Together. That somehow seeing this, all the demons of Ryan's past had been exorcised. As if someone had come into this once abandoned home and filled it with love and proved that a home could be made anywhere out of anything.

Ryan returned from his walk that night with a new-found hope. If that family could make his old house a home, then he and Theresa could make this work and start their *own* family.

9

At seven-thirty in the morning, Marissa tiptoed across the marble foyer of Caleb's house. She had spent the night out. Again. With DJ . . . the yard guy. He was edgy and dangerous in ways that meant he wasn't a part of Newport. In ways that reminded her of Ryan. He was the outsider who didn't belong. He worked. He drove a beat-up truck. And the best part for Marissa was that he was a secret and he was hers. For the last week she had snuck out of her house every night to go over to his place.

Marissa went into her bedroom and changed into her bathing suit, then she threw a tank top and skirt on top of it and headed back downstairs. In the kitchen her mom was eating breakfast with Caleb.

"Morning, Marissa," Julie said in a sickly sweet voice. "You're up early."

"Yeah, I . . ." And she tried to think of an excuse her mom would buy. Something so that her mom would not discover that she had been out all night. "I just wanted to make sure I got all the sun."

"Good. You were starting to look a little washed out. You look so much better when you're tan. Tan is the black of summer. Totally slimming."

"Thanks," Marissa said as she went to the fridge and poured herself a glass of the freshly squeezed orange juice that she was sure her mom had made one of Caleb's maids prepare that morning.

She took a sip, then looked outside the window where she could see DJ setting up his equipment for work that day.

Caleb looked at Marissa, then looked out the window as well and saw DJ. He stood up quickly. "Damn that kid."

Marissa shuddered and quickly turned from the window. Did Caleb know the truth? Had he seen her sneak through the house this morning?

Marissa sat at the table with her orange juice and pretended to read the *Orange County Register*.

Caleb turned to Julie. "That's the third time this week that boy's been late."

"Why don't you just fire him, Cal? I'm sure there are plenty just like him out there. They're always hanging out by Home Depot. I could pick one up on the way home from yogalates."

Marissa almost choked on her orange juice. Was DJ going to get fired because of her? She glared at her mother.

"What?" Julie snapped.

"Nothing. I just wouldn't be so quick to judge." *Or fire.* She whispered under her breath.

116

"When did you become such an advocate for the working man?"

"I didn't. I'm just saying."

"He's the gardener, Marissa. Not a doctor."

"Fine," Marissa said and went back to sipping her orange juice and reading the paper.

But Caleb continued to look out the window and back at Marissa. And Marissa was sure she was about to get caught.

"No. Marissa's right. The working man deserves a shot. Like the rest of us."

"Really?" Marissa asked, completely thrown by Caleb's generosity.

"Really, Cal?" Julie asked, also thrown.

"Yes. They are the force that keeps this community going. Juju, who would do your laundry and clean your house if it weren't for them?"

"Good point, Cal. I knew there was a reason I married you."

For your money, Marissa thought but didn't say a word.

"Doesn't mean I can't give him a warning, though." And Caleb stood up from the table and went down to the yard, where Marissa watched him approach DJ.

Marissa stood by the window and watched as Caleb yelled at DJ. She winced at the harsh words she could faintly hear, but she couldn't save him. If she did she would have to admit that they had a relationship. She wasn't ready to give up her escape.

DJ looked up to the window and Marissa caught his eyes with hers. They screamed for help, but Marissa couldn't do it. She wasn't ready to give him away. Not yet. She liked him.

DJ had gone for the evening by the time Marissa decided to come inside after spending the day lying by the pool. Summer and Zach were throwing a small barbecue on his father's yacht and sailing down to Emerald Bay to watch the sun set, and Marissa had promised Summer that she would go, even though she knew it would be another Newport party. She gathered up her magazines and towel and made her way back to the house. As she passed by the giant glass windows, she looked at her reflection. Her skin had turned a golden brown and her face was framed by sun-kissed strands of hair. She was the quintessential California beauty, but she still felt like a fraud. She didn't like being here. In Newport. In this mansion.

As Marissa entered the house, she heard her mom and Kaitlin returning from a day of shopping. The rustling of bags made Marissa cringe. She wasn't in the mood to hear about everything her mom and sister had bought that day. Marissa quickly made her way up to her room and shut the door behind her. She remembered when she was Kaitlin's age and she used to go shopping with her mom and return home with bags full of new clothes. When she used to run up to her room and excitedly try on every new purchase for her dad. And she would prance around the house like a princess and her dad would tell her how beautiful she was. But now as she stood alone in her room in this horror of a house, Marissa knew this would never happen again. She missed her dad. She missed when they were all a family, when her mom wasn't so vindictive and money-grubbing. When they had nothing to worry about. When everything was perfect.

Marissa had showered and was trying on clothes when Kaitlin knocked on the door and entered, wearing a new dress.

"Look how cute," Kaitlin exclaimed as she entered her sister's room and twirled around.

"Cute," Marissa said without enthusiasm.

"Wait till you see the rest," Kaitlin exclaimed as she ran off in a hurry.

"Kaitlin, don't —" But Kaitlin was already out the door. "— come back," Marissa finished to herself. "I have to go."

But Kaitlin quickly returned in another completely new outfit. Again, Marissa was unenthusiastic, but this time Kaitlin noticed.

"I feel like a princess," Kaitlin started. Then crossed to Marissa's balcony and stood out in the summer breeze. "Look, I am a princess," she said as she hung her head over the side of the balcony. "Like Rapunzel." And Marissa wanted to tell her sister to get out of her room, but held back. For a moment she felt bad. Kaitlin didn't have Jimmy around like she did when she was younger, and she knew that Kaitlin missed this. Maybe Kaitlin even hated being here as much as she did.

"You do look like a princess," Marissa said. "Except . . ."

"Except what?" Kaitlin asked, worried.

"Except you need a necklace," Marissa answered and went over to her dresser. She pulled out a gold necklace from her jewelry box — one that her dad had given her when she was Kaitlin's age. "Here. Borrow this."

Kaitlin reached out for the necklace and fastened it around her neck. "Thanks," she said and smiled at Marissa.

"You're welcome. Now go and . . ." But Marissa was interrupted by Julie entering.

"Marissa. How cute are your sister's clothes?" Julie asked as she went to Kaitlin and inspected her outfit. "Oh, but this necklace. All wrong. Take that off." And Julie unfastened the necklace from Kaitlin's neck and placed it on Marissa's dresser. "Where did you get this?"

"Marissa let me —" Kaitlin started as she reached for the necklace again.

"Hideous, come on. You can borrow one of mine. It's got bigger diamonds," Julie said as she led Kaitlin out the door.

"Oh, Marissa, I forgot." Julie poked her head back into the room. "I got you a new dress, too. It's

120

in my closet. You can have it when you promise not to wear that vile thing you bought last week."

"Thanks," Marissa said sarcastically. She picked up the necklace on her dresser and held it in her hands. A reminder of happier times. A reminder of her father.

Kaitlin peeked her head back into Marissa's room. "Sorry." Marissa didn't say anything. "It's just the way she is, you know?"

Marissa nodded as her sister slipped inside the room and gently closed the door behind her. Marissa just looked at Kaitlin. *What?* The two sisters hadn't really talked at all since they moved into Caleb's mansion.

"Are you going to defend her now?" Marissa said finally.

"No," Kaitlin answered quickly. "I wanted to tell you that I'm leaving."

"Good," Marissa said as she eyed the door, waiting for her sister to leave.

"I mean in the fall. I'm going to boarding school."

"What?" Marissa asked, utterly confused. How come her sister got to leave this town and not her? "How . . ."

"I asked Mom. I don't think I can go through high school here. Go through the same things . . ."

"As I did," Marissa finished, now understanding, realizing that her sister looked up to her. Saw all the things she'd gone through.

"Yeah." Her sister nodded. "It all seems too hard."

"Yeah," Marissa said softly, wanting to say more, but she was interrupted by Julie yelling for Kaitlin from down the hall.

"I should go," Kaitlin said as she turned toward the door.

With that, Kaitlin was out the door and gone. The door shut and Marissa stood alone in her room. She took the necklace her dad had given her and placed it around her own neck. An attempt to save the past.

Marissa sat at the bow of the boat sipping champagne as the wind blew through her hair. Summer and Zach and all his friends were in the back drinking and smoking cigars. The motor hummed softly as Zach maneuvered the boat out of the harbor past the giant yachts that sat off the backyards of some of Newport's richest. Their giant mansions sat on grassy knolls in Linda Isle and their homes were worth millions. Marissa gazed at the homes as they passed by, wondering if the people who lived inside felt like she did in Caleb's mansion. If they called their mansions home, or if they were just houses to show off their wealth. A signal to the community that they had made it behind the Orange curtain. Marissa watched as a little boy kicked his soccer ball in the backyard of one of the mansions. He was alone but he had his own game. He would kick the ball far ahead of himself and then run up and kick it back to where he had come from. A one-man game of soccer. One versus one instead of the usual eleven. But the boy did not look happy, and Marissa wondered what it would be like to live in Newport in a giant mansion with no friends. And for a moment she thought she understood. She looked back at Summer and saw her talking to Zach, and she looked down at the water and saw her feet dangling all alone. No one to play with. And she wondered if this was it. If this was all that life had to offer. A one-on-one soccer game or a life of sipping champagne and smoking cigars on the front of a thirty-foot yacht.

"Coop," Summer yelled from behind her. "What are you doing by yourself? Come back here. Zach found a bottle of his dad's Dom. We're going to open it."

Marissa reluctantly stood up and slowly made her way to the back. The boat rocked back and forth as Zach shut off the engine and Marissa found a seat in the back.

Zach and his friends hoisted the mainsail as they moved out of the harbor and the boat picked up speed. The evening wind rustled hard against their backs and they moved out into the Pacific Ocean. Alongside the boat several dolphins played in the wake, their fins appearing every few seconds as they came up for air. Marissa watched as their soft skin glided through the water so free and alive.

Summer came over and sat next to Marissa as they picked up even more speed and headed south to Emerald Bay.

Emerald Bay was a series of coves that sat just

at the edge of Laguna Niguel. During the day, a lot of Newporters sailed down and anchored in the coves so that they could swim into shore and enjoy the pristine beaches that were accessible only to the privileged few, those who had even more money than most of Newport, who lived there. At night the coves were fairly empty and quiet, and the sea was calm within them.

As they approached one of the coves, Zach and his friends lowered the sail and allowed the boat to slowly drift in the cool waters. Summer grabbed the bottle of Dom as Zach lowered the anchor and the boat held still inside the cove.

Everyone gathered at the back of the boat, and Summer handed the bottle of champagne to Zach.

He held up the bottle and popped the cork so that it sprayed out into the ocean. "To new friends," he said as he winked at Summer and she held up her glass to be filled with the bubbly liquid.

Zach poured champagne into everyone's glasses, and the new friends sat around and drank and talked. But Marissa was bored and didn't have much to say. Zach and his friends were carrying on about politics and money and things that Marissa thought people her age didn't care about — or even really understand. At least she didn't, but she watched as Summer pretended to be interested.

And she came to the realization that everyone in Newport was hiding behind a facade. That everyone was just putting on a show to fit in. She looked at Zach, who was like a young Kennedy, strong features and great manners. The kind of guy every mother in Newport wants their daughter to bring home. The kind of guy who ends up being president one day, or a senator at least. And she looked at Summer, who had spent all of last year pretending that she wasn't part of the Newport scene, that she was smarter and more cultured so that she and Seth would have something in common. But now, even as Marissa watched, her friend was falling back into the traps of the Newport scene. The money, the power, the facade. And she knew that she *really* didn't fit in. She felt like she had seen what was beyond Newport, beyond Orange County, and she wasn't sure she wanted to return. And the reality of Ryan in Chino with Theresa and the unborn baby just made Marissa realize even more that the rest of the world was different. And she wanted to leave.

Just as the sun set over the ocean and the purple and pink and orange turned to black lit by the moon, Zach pulled up anchor and they motored back to Newport. The stars of the night a guide back to their homes. To the harbor that protected them from the outside world.

When they docked in the marina, Marissa went belowdeck and gathered her things, her purse and her car keys, and got ready to get off the boat.

"Coop, where you going? We're going to stay. Hang out. I think we might all just crash here under the stars."

And as fun and exotic as that sounded, Marissa knew she had to go. She couldn't be here. She was sick of pretending like she belonged.

"I'm going to go home. But you should stay. That sounds really —"

"Romantic? I know. Do you care? I don't want you to have to go by yourself."

"I'm fine, Sum. Really. Stay. Have fun."

"Sure?" Summer asked with hesitation.

But Marissa just nodded yes and leaped off the boat.

As Marissa drove home, she thought about her life, her past and her future. How she didn't want to go back to Caleb's mansion. She drove slowly back up the coast and stared at all the homes as they passed by her window and thought about all the happy families eating dinner inside. And then Marissa passed by a sign for a new development that had recently been completed. She stared at the sign. There was something about it that caught her attention, and it wasn't the Newport Group insignia at the bottom. The insignia of Caleb's company. She pulled her car over and entered the community, drawn by some unseen force, some voice inside of her that told her to go this way. And as she drove through the community of new homes memories flooded back. This was the location of her first real encounter with Ryan and Seth. Her first step to leaving Newport behind. She found the once-burned model home where Ryan had stayed and she parked outside, letting her emotions wash over her.

From where her car was parked she could see inside the home, into the dining room, where a young family sat eating dinner. And she realized that she had been right, that there were happy families inside some of these homes, and she thought about her own family. How she had barely seen her father over the summer. How Caleb had blackmailed her into living with him. How Julie criticized her every move. And how Ryan had left.

And she thought about Ryan, about the first time they had really bonded. It was at the edge of the unfinished pool of the very house that sat in front of her now. There they had opened up to each other, told each other about their troubles, their worries, how their families were falling apart. And Marissa remembered the night that she had left one of Holly's parties to come see Ryan and how she had asked him to let her stay and he had told her to go. And she remembered the song that had played that night. The hallelujah that echoed over and over. Jeff Buckley's song. And she remembered how she had made him a CD called the Model Home Mix, and how it had burned in the fire that Luke had started and how after she had slept with Luke she had made Ryan a new one. How she had never given it to him. How she had told him it was too late.

But now Marissa searched through her car and found that CD. The one that had never made it into

Ryan's hands. And she put it in and forwarded to that song.

Jeff Buckley's "Hallelujah" poured through her speakers, and as she watched the happy young family inside the house enjoy dinner, tears ran down her face.

She drove away with the song on repeat. The hallelujahs continued as her tear-filled eyes managed to navigate the streets of Newport, and she made her way to DJ's house.

She would go to him so that she could escape — at least for a night.

Marissa stood at his window and tapped three times lightly so as not to wake his parents. DJ drew the shades and saw her standing there alone, cheeks stained with tears. He smiled and came to the door to let her in.

"What's wrong?" he asked.

"I can't do this anymore," she cried and fell into DJ's arms. "I don't belong here."

"I know, but do any of us?" he said, wiping a tear from her cheek.

Marissa nodded yes. "But everyone else seems to fit. . . ." Her voice trailed off as she thought about Summer and Zach and his friends. How they enjoyed Newport. How they were probably still on Zach's yacht, drinking. Having fun.

"I don't," DJ said.

Marissa pulled back from his shoulder and kissed him. *Thank you.*

And for a while Marissa felt numb again, like she had escaped all the pressures of Newport. That she had run out of Caleb's mansion. That the memory of Ryan had turned soft and bearable. That her heart was no longer aching.

Later DJ kissed her forehead and she fell asleep in his arms. She felt safe.

The next morning when Marissa awoke she found herself alone, and she panicked. Had DJ left her? But he returned at that moment with a rose and some orange juice. Marissa kissed him and smiled. She sipped her juice and realized that it was not freshly squeezed and this made her smile even more. She was no longer a prisoner in Caleb's hell.

She turned to DJ, about to thank him, but found him gazing at her longingly. And she worried, did he want more?

10

They hitchhiked. Twenty-five miles from the shores of Astoria to Cannon Beach. Cali and Seth had found an older couple who looked like they had just come from a Grateful Dead show. The inside of their car smelled of patchouli and the faint smell of marijuana lingered on the cloth seats of their 1980 Buick.

Cali had stood on the side of the road with her thumb in the air. A dare given her by Seth. He didn't believe that people could still hitchhike. That anyone really picked up hitchhikers anymore. He thought that was a part of history. A part of an era in time that had long since passed. But Cali had been determined to prove him wrong, to show him that the world was not all he made it out to be. That beyond the coast of Southern California and outside of a dingy Greyhound bus, there was a world he had never experienced. A world she wanted to introduce to him. And Seth had accepted her challenge.

"If you can get someone to pick us up," Seth had said to her, "then I'll believe you."

And now as they sat in the back of the Buick, Seth looked at Cali and believed. There was a world beyond Newport, beyond Portland, and he was happy to experience it.

As the car bounced along the road and the couple played old recordings of various Dead shows, Seth thought about his new life. And he devised a new plan.

He'd spent most of his life alone, always trying to fit in, but never quite getting there. And he'd accepted his status as an outsider. And over the past year, that status had actually gained him popularity; his quirkiness and quick wit had finally charmed his friends and gotten him the girl. But Seth had always thought of himself in relation to everyone else. In relation to Summer, would she like him? Did she love him? In relation to Ryan, would they become friends? Brothers? In relation to Marissa, had they become friends? A neighbor who never said a word to him most of his life? Friends? Over the past year Seth had discovered himself in terms of everyone else. He had discovered his role among this group of friends, but Seth hadn't taken the time to discover who *he* was. Without any of his friends around. Without his parents.

And as he looked at Cali, who had closed her eyes and was feeling the beat of the music, he thought how grateful he was to meet someone new. Someone who had lived a life different from any he had ever known. And he was glad to be here in the back of the car with people he had never met in his entire life.

This was what life outside the Newport bubble was like, he thought, all those things he had over-heard his dad talking about.

"I'm liking this music," Seth said as he leaned forward and spoke to the couple in the front.

"You want a joint?" the woman asked. "It's better that way."

"No thanks," Seth said, sitting back. "Isn't that illegal?" Cali glared at him. "Oh, sorry, medicinal. Right. I forgot that law. Do you think I can get this for my iPod?"

The woman in the front just stared at Seth. *What are you talking about?*

Seth pulled his iPod from his backpack. "Music. You know."

But the man just turned up the stereo and took a hit off the woman's joint.

Seth looked at Cali, *what?* But Cali just shook her head and laughed. Then placed her hand on Seth's, as if to say *relax.*

So Seth sat back in his seat and listened to the guitar cry endlessly with the beat of the drums and the keyboards. The soft sound of their voices. The Dead.

Cali smiled at him and placed his iPod back in his bag. Then she whispered, "Just experience it."

And Seth smiled and watched out the window

as the ocean and the rocks and the sand passed by him. A visual accompaniment to the sounds coming from the car's speakers. He relaxed and went with it.

The couple continued to smoke their joint. The usual narration that went on in Seth's head, the voice that would normally ramble on about the legality of marijuana and then its medicinal effects, finally shut off and Seth was able to just listen to the music and enjoy the view. Enjoy the fact that he was thousands of miles from Newport. Away from the world he'd always hated, and now here he was, listening to music he'd never really heard before, and driving in a car with two old hippies who were stoned out of their minds.

But there was something about sitting next to Cali that made Seth believe that he would be just fine. That when he was with her, he was calm and cool. And didn't need a plan. With Cali, he felt completely out of control yet completely powerful.

"Cannon Beach," the woman said as she put out her joint and the old man pulled the car onto the shoulder of the road.

"Thank you so much," Cali said as she opened her door and climbed out.

"Peace," Seth said as he held up two fingers and hopped out of the car.

"Okay, you crack me up," Cali said as they sat on the beach eating sandwiches they had bought from a local deli.

"Why?" Seth asked. "I am a very mature and serious being." He took a bite of his sandwich and washed it down with a sip of soda.

"In the car? The iPod?"

"What? The Dead deserve the chance to be heard by everyone. I was just trying to bring them up to speed. It's the twenty-first century. We have technology now. CDs. I don't have a tape player. I cannot download music from a tape deck into my computer or my iPod."

"Fine. You got me there. But the medicinal marijuana?"

"Hey, I'm from California. My grandma has cancer. I know how these things work."

"Your grandma smokes pot?"

"No. She lives in New York. But I'm sure if she could get it she would. Maybe I should send her some. Do you have any more in your backpack?"

"Seth!" Cali exclaimed as she pulled her bag out of his reach.

"What? Just asking."

The two continued to eat their sandwiches as the coastal fog cleared and the sun beat down on them. Its brightness reflecting off of the cool ocean water.

Seth lay back and soaked up the sun, his pale skin slowly turning brown. Cali lay down next to him and they watched the clouds move quickly above them.

The sky turned white and blue and bright. Seth let the sand slide through his fingers. Thoughts of home rushed through his mind. Thoughts of being here in Cannon Beach, the small-town artists' colony, thoughts of traveling the world with Cali, thoughts of the Wards' house, thoughts of Newport, and Seth wondered what it all meant.

Where did he belong?

Truly.

Forever.

For the last few weeks he had thought that he belonged in Portland, but now after his trip with Cali, he wondered if he wasn't supposed to spend the rest of his life traveling, experiencing everything. Seeing new sights. Meeting new people.

He looked over at her. Her sea-green eyes were wide open and staring, taking in the sky above her. Maybe. He thought and took the sight of her in. But maybe not.

Then his mind went back to racing like it always did. He was Seth Cohen, after all, and he needed a plan.

The ocean waves bounced gently on the sand, slowly rolling toward their feet. But the tide had not come in yet and so they stayed dry. Seth's mind raced. Thoughts of a plan developed.

He needed experience, he thought. Donald Trump didn't become a multibillionaire because he opened one business and succeeded. No, he opened one after the other, he had his money invested everywhere, he even jumped on the reality-show bandwagon. Talk about experience.

All he needed to do was travel around the

world. Or at least the country. Take Cali with him, experience life on his own. Away from his parents or anyone who could act like his parents. Go out and see the world.

Seth turned over and looked at Cali. He was ready to present her with his plan. They were going on the road.

"I've got a plan," he started.

Cali sat up and looked at him. Attentive.

"Let's just keep on going. Traveling. See where our thumbs take us."

Cali placed her hand on Seth's shoulder. Consoling. And then she preemptively cut him off. "That's sweet but I was thinking, too. I'm just going to stay here. Learn to blow glass. Open a gallery. I don't know. I'm tired of moving around. I want to settle down, find a home."

"What about home being everywhere and everyone?"

"I was stoned. You understand."

But Seth didn't understand. Things seemed so good between them. Their friendship seemed stronger than ever. He never expected this. He *had* a plan.

Cali took her hand off his shoulder, then kissed his forehead as she stood up and gathered her things.

"You're just going to leave? Just like that?"

"If anyone would understand, it's you."

"But," Seth started, then stopped himself. She was right. He'd done the same thing to Summer.

Just up and left. No explanation. Nothing. And then he thought about karma. Was the world trying to tell him something? Had he made a mistake?

Cali continued walking away from him, and Seth thought about his life.

This was like *On the Road*. Friends came and went. The experiences changed day by day. And sometimes Sal Paradise found himself alone.

"How am I going to get back?" he yelled after her.

"Hitchhike. It's good for you. See you, Cohen."

And sometimes Seth Cohen found himself alone.

Seth stood on the side of the road, his thumb in the air. Waiting. This wasn't as easy to do as when he had Cali with him. Apparently, he thought, after walking for an hour, hitchhiking was only alive and well today if you had a pretty girl with you.

All he needed was a ride to a town called Banks, just fifty or so miles from where he had started. He'd called Luke once Cali had left him, and Luke had agreed to come out and get him that afternoon, but with traffic and all, they agreed that it might be easier if they met halfway. That way Seth could be back home in time for work the following day. Besides, Seth had wanted to try hitchhiking again. But now as he stood here alone with his thumb in the air, he realized that it might have been easier to have Luke drive all the way out to get him.

He wanted to turn back, but at this point he was far enough down the road that it wasn't worth it. That it would just make the whole trip take much longer.

Several cars whizzed past Seth, ignoring his plea for a ride.

"Damn it," he shouted as he kicked some gravel on the side of the road. This was going to take forever.

Seth was ready to give up and turn around, find the nearest phone and call Luke and wait for him there, when he saw a sign posted to a tree. IF YOU LIVED HERE, YOU'D BE HOME BY NOW. But he didn't live there. And he wasn't home.

Seth was confused. He'd seen signs like this outside of cities where traffic lasted for hours, but he'd never seen a sign like this in a rural area, where it appeared there *were* no homes, and no people living anywhere.

Straying off the road, Seth approached the sign and stared at it in awe, utterly confused. Was this supposed to be a sign? Was he supposed to run off and live in the woods? Was this the experience he was looking for? Did he have to go alone?

Then Seth got closer and read the fine print under the sign. It was a recruitment poster for the Forest Preserve. They wanted people to come live with them and protect the environment. Fight for a cause.

Seth looked at the sign and laughed. At least

he knew where his home was not. He continued walking, more determined than ever to go back to Portland.

Finally, after Seth had been walking for another thirty minutes, and his hair was completely curly from the humid air, and his mouth was parched, a car slowed down beside him.

"Hey," a guy just a few years older than Seth said as the car stopped next to him. "I've seen you at Burnside before. Hop in, man."

Seth looked up and recognized the passenger who was talking. He was one of the really good skateboarders he had watched in the park.

"Yeah, I've been there. I'm Seth," Seth said as he hopped in the back of their car. Most of the backseat was covered in skateboarding magazines, decks to boards, wheels, a skateboarder's paradise. Seth stared in awe.

The driver looked back and saw Seth staring at all the equipment.

"Hey, I'm Guy. You like any of that stuff? Take whatever you want. We get free shit all the time."

"Really?" Seth asked.

"Yeah, man. The companies all like to give you free crap so that one day when you're famous, you'll say you learned to ride on their boards. But we got plenty. Seriously, take a deck. Or two."

"Thanks," Seth said as he rummaged through the equipment.

"I'm Tony, by the way."

Seth shook his hand, and Guy started the engine. The dust of the road billowed behind them as they drove away.

"So, what's your story?" Tony asked as Seth grabbed one of the decks and placed it on his lap. He'd found the one he was going to keep. The underside was yellow with a picture of a girl on a table. A magician's act. The caption said SEE A LIVE BEAUTIFUL WOMAN SAWED IN HALF.

"Well," Seth began, ready to give his long expanded Seth Cohen version of the story. Ready to tell the guys how he had run away from home in his boat, then ended up with one of his old enemies who had become his friend, and he was living with his friend's gay dad and his lover. And he had just been left by a girl in the middle of nowhere. But Seth decided to restrain himself. Try something new. "Seeing the world, boys. Taking one day at a time."

"You headed back to Portland?" Guy asked.

"Yes. No," Seth said with confusion as he remembered that Luke was picking him up in Banks. "A friend of mine is meeting me in Banks. If that's cool. If you guys are going there. Oh, no. I never asked. Did I?" Seth started to panic. He wasn't good at hitchhiking.

"It's cool. We'll head there and then I think we're going to head up north and check out a skate park in Vancouver."

"Cool," Seth said, clutching the deck of the skateboard in his lap.

* * *

Luke met Seth at one of the oldest gas stations in Banks.

"So, no one pumps their own gas here?" Seth asked.

Luke and Seth sat inside the car as the attendant filled Luke's car with gas. Seth flipped his new skateboard deck in his hands.

"It's the law," Luke replied.

"And I thought Newport was strange. Elitist. But this? This is better than valet parking at South Coast Plaza."

Luke gave Seth a strange look.

"Not that I would know. I've just heard."

Luke just nodded, then drove away once he had paid the attendant.

The traffic from the city was pretty backed up, but the road heading back in was fairly clear.

Seth plugged his iPod into the truck's system and put on some of his music. He was glad to be back with Luke. Back with someone he knew.

"I've got news for you, Cohen."

Seth looked at Luke, *yeah?*

"Remember Amanda?"

"You two?" Seth turned down the music.

Luke nodded yes.

"So you have a girlfriend?"

"No, Cohen. Just playing the game. But let's just say if this were soccer, she'd be my striker."

"Speaking to the layman here. The emo geek. Don't play sports, remember?"

"Right. She's like my lead singer in the band."

"Lead singer," Seth said, nodding. "That's pretty heavy. Has she played your guitar?"

"I don't play and tell."

"Touché."

"So what happened to Cali? She just up and left?"

"Karma, my friend. Karma," Seth said, remembering Cali's last words. That he would be the only one to understand why she needed to go out on her own. That he had done the same thing to Summer.

Back in Portland, Seth sat in his room unpacking his bag. Thinking about Cali. About karma. How she had just up and left. And then he thought about Summer, how he had done the same thing to her. And he felt guilty and horrible and he wanted to call and apologize and let her know that he understood why she was mad. That he hoped she would understand.

That he understood. That when Cali left, he got it. He understood that she needed to find her home. Her center.

And he hoped that Summer would see that he was trying to do the same. That his leaving her wasn't in vain.

But as he stared at the phone, wondering if he should call, he realized that she would never understand. That he had given her no reason to. That he had just left without any sort of explanation.

The phone screamed at him and he jumped. It was ringing. He picked it up.

"Hello?" he said. Hoping fate and karma had come back to him, and it was Summer.

"Seth," the voice said sternly. And Seth's mouth clenched. His fingers tightened. It was his mother.

"Mother," he responded.

"It's the Fourth of July next weekend," she said.

"I know."

"Well, your dad and I are helping Caleb and Julie throw a party and we want you to come back. For the holiday."

Seth thought for a moment. The Fourth was always fun in Newport. The town went crazy. But still, if he went back then he'd have to face Summer and his parents. There was no way he could just slip in and out of town. He'd be stuck.

"You can go back to Portland. Just come home for the weekend."

"I don't think I can," Seth said. "I already promised Luke and his dad and these friends of ours."

"Please, Seth," she pleaded. Seth could hear the hurt in his mother's voice. But this wasn't about her. This was about him. The summer of Seth.

"I made plans," he said, then hung up the phone. "I love you," he whispered, once the receiver was down.

He couldn't go back to Newport, not yet. He still needed to know. Where was his home?

11

The Fourth of July holiday had approached seemingly out of nowhere, but still Ryan found himself at work. He needed the extra pay and if he worked the holiday he got paid double overtime. Of course, today turned out to be the hottest day of the summer. As the temperature approached one hundred, Ryan took off his shirt and let the sun beat down on him. Each nail hammered was another diaper for the baby or a meal on the table. The echo of the hammer was solitary and lonely, followed only by the sound of two men below, sawing pieces of wood. All the other workers had taken the holiday and gone home to be with their families and their friends.

Ryan wiped the sweat from his brow and thought about Theresa. Her mom was throwing a small party in the backyard for the holiday, and her brother was stopping by with some of their other relatives. He wondered if she was pretending that things were okay, and he thought how great it would be once he got home from work today to tell her that they could stop pretending. That things really were going to be okay.

The past day or so, Ryan had been riding high on his realization that a home could be made out of anything. After he had seen the happy family in his old house, he'd realized that he and Theresa could make this work. They could be a family.

Ryan hadn't said anything to Theresa yet for fear that things might go awry as they always seemed to over the past week. He was waiting for the right time. But he had hope that today she would be in a good mood. That after a day with her family where they got to hang out and reconnect, she would be happy to see him.

The day dragged on forever. Even though Ryan was only working until three, just a little more than half a day, he felt like he had been there for two days by the time he was released.

Ryan took his time riding back to Theresa's as his mind wandered all over the place. He thought about Marissa back in Newport, and he wondered what she was doing. If Caleb and her mom, or the Cohens, were throwing a giant Newport affair. Would he have been invited if he had still been in Newport? And he wondered what kind of fireworks display the city had, if they showed off their wealth then, too. And he wondered if anyone there had to work on a holiday, if anyone needed the extra money to pay for an unborn child, a child they had accepted responsibility for whether or not it was their own. But he doubted it.

And he thought about Seth, who would be spending the holiday in Portland with Luke and Luke's dad. And he wondered if they would be out on Seth's boat setting off their own fireworks, or if they had sailed somewhere for the weekend. He could picture Luke excited to set off his own fireworks, and Seth reading the instructions to him, cautioning him of the dangers and the possibility of fire and dismemberment, even death. And Ryan laughed at the image of the two of them together. How had Seth ended up in Portland anyway?

But then Ryan thought of his own holiday plans, and how he was so excited to get home and tell Theresa that everything was going to be okay. That his old house had turned into a home, that they could do it, too.

And he had hope.

Ryan thought about what he would say, his plan, how he would tell her what he had seen the other night. And they would reminisce about how he used to run from his old house and hide out with her, and he would tell her how happy the young family had looked, that there was hope for them. But then Ryan got nervous. What if she didn't believe him? What if she didn't care? He decided he needed something more and he turned his bike to the right and rode to the strip mall down the street.

*   *   *

The parking lot was full of people buying last-minute provisions for their Fourth of July barbecues. Ryan rode through the mess of cars and parked his bike outside the little grocery store.

Inside, Ryan meandered aimlessly up and down the aisles, not exactly sure what it was he was looking for — pickles? M&M's? What could he buy that would make Theresa believe him that everything was going to turn out fine? Then, as he passed by the baby aisle, Ryan saw a young father with a bouquet of flowers in one hand and a bag of diapers in the other. And as he looked closer he realized that it was the same young father he had spied in his old house the other night, one third of the family that had given Ryan hope.

"Hey," Ryan said, approaching the man.

"Hey," the father said softly as he looked at Ryan quickly then returned to the baby food.

"For the baby?" Ryan asked.

"Yeah, man."

Ryan picked up a bag of diapers. "Me too."

The father stared at Ryan as Ryan stood there uneasy. He wanted to ask the father a million questions. All the questions he hadn't been able to ask his own father. How he'd made it? Was the baby his? Was he truly happy? Did he ever have to pretend? How was his old room? Was the house nice now? Did he love his home, his family?

But instead all Ryan could ask was, "Where'd you get the flowers?"

The father looked at Ryan, then replied, "There's

a guy on the corner out there as you enter the parking lot. He's selling them."

"Thanks," Ryan said as the father quickly made his way out of the store. Probably freaked out by Ryan.

Ryan looked down at the bag of diapers he was still holding. His hand was shaking, worn from the hard, hot day at work and trembling from the fear he still had of becoming a father.

But now, at least, he knew what to get Theresa. He put the bag of diapers back on the shelf and made his way to the front of the store, but as he was about to walk out, the glass case full of cigarettes caught his eye.

If we think our lives are bad now, imagine if we didn't have luck.

Theresa's words entered his head. Her saying. Her belief dating back to when they were younger, when they were friends. When they used to sit on her porch smoking and talking and planning their futures. When she would take his packs of cigarettes and turn one over for good luck.

Ryan went to the back of the checkout line. He knew what else he needed to ensure that things really would work out between them. Luck.

So he stood at the back of the line, his skin a dark brown against his white and dusty T-shirt, and he waited his turn. He didn't care that he wasn't eighteen. That he had been asked for his ID the last time he had been in the store. He would beg. Plead if he had to. He needed the cigarettes. The luck.

Ryan messed with his hair and straightened his shirt, trying to appear older than he really was. Trying to appear like an adult.

Then it was Ryan's turn.

"A pack of lights," he said with a sideways glance, trying not to let the cashier see his eyes, lest she ask him for his identification. To prove his age.

He needed the cigarettes.

The cashier went to the glass case and pulled out the white pack of cigarettes.

"That's six-fifty," she said. "You want a bag?"

"No, thanks," Ryan replied, handing her the money.

"Happy Fourth of July."

"You too," Ryan said as he picked up the cigarettes with a smile and walked out the door. He'd done it. His luck was changing.

Outside the store, Ryan removed the plastic covering off the top of the white cardboard. Then he turned the pack of cigarettes over and beat them against his rough calloused hands. Packing them. Then as he stood there watching all the families run in and out of the store, he reached inside the pack of cigarettes and pulled one out. The lucky one. And he returned it to the pack upside down, so that the tobacco stared back at him from inside the cardboard box.

They would have luck now, and their lives would never be as bad as they had imagined.

Ryan got on his bike and rode over to the man

who was selling the flowers at the entrance to the parking lot.

"The roses, please," Ryan said, then pointed at a bouquet of red roses.

The man handed Ryan the flowers, and Ryan handed over the last bit of cash he had on him.

Ryan rode off with the flowers in his hand and the cigarettes in his pocket. He had spent more money than he should, but Ryan didn't mind. It was worth it. His luck was changing.

Back at Theresa's house, most of her family and friends had gathered for the holiday celebration. Her backyard was full of people. Tables were covered with bowls of chips and salsa and guacamole. Coolers were full of beer and sodas. And a barbecue was smoking with hamburgers and hot dogs.

Ryan left his bike in front of the house and came bounding through the front door. The bouquet of flowers bouncing in his hand and the pack of cigarettes tight inside his pocket.

He found Theresa out back.

"Happy Fourth," he said. She smiled as she took the flowers from his hand and held them up to her face. Enjoying the scent, their beauty. Ryan watched as the smile radiated through her body. Things really were changing, he thought.

"They're beautiful," Theresa said as she leaned forward and gave Ryan a kiss on the cheek. Ryan felt her elation, but watched it die as she handed the flowers back to him and said, "Can you put them inside in some water?"

Ryan took the flowers back in his hands and was about to go inside, when he felt the pack of cigarettes pressing against his thigh. She wasn't going to get away this easily. He had the luck. The confidence. To tell her that he'd had a revelation. That things were going to work out and he wanted to put an end to the pretending.

"Come with me," he pleaded.

"I've got my family," Theresa protested, gesturing at the crowd of people in her backyard.

"For just a minute," Ryan said, then gave her his brooding look. The look that he used when he wanted something.

"Don't do that," she said, pushing his head forward, making his eyes look her straight on.

"Come on," he pleaded again, then grabbed her hand and started to walk away. She pulled back, but Ryan squeezed harder.

"Fine, but only for a few minutes," she said reluctantly.

Once inside, Ryan sat Theresa down at the kitchen table as he put the roses in a vase.

"What's with you?" she asked as he continued to cut the stems of the roses.

"I . . ." he started, then paused. He hadn't really thought about what he was going to say. How he was going to explain everything that he saw.

About the father in the store today. The happy family that had moved into his old house. Would she even see that as a sign? He didn't know where to start. "Nothing," he said, then smiled at her.

"Okay."

Ryan put the vase of flowers on the table and sat in the chair next to her. Theresa just stared at him. An awkward silence fell between them. Her hand reached out and touched the soft petals. She pulled one off. *He loves me? He loves me not?* Ryan thought as she held the petal in her hand.

Was she testing him?

Figuring everything out.

He loves you. Ryan smiled. She was his best friend and she always would be. And now they would have a family.

Theresa crushed the petal between her fingers, moving it back and forth until her skin had turned red. Ryan watched patiently. Then smiled at her. *He loves you, I promise.*

"Let's go," Ryan said as he stood up and grabbed her hand. He couldn't allow her to continue to pick off the petals of the roses one by one. The chance that she would land on *not*. That the last petal would ruin things forever. That their family would be doomed. "I have something to show you."

Theresa stood up and let the remains of the petal fall from her fingers, its crumbs of red dusting upon the table.

* * *

Outside, Ryan held Theresa's hand as he led her through the neighborhood. Past the fence they used to jump as a shortcut to his house. Past Mr. Ramirez and his two daughters. Past the houses they had hidden behind in an attempt to outrun the ghetto birds. Past their childhood.

Ryan let the softness of her hand rest firmly in his own.

The white sidewalk cracked and gave as they walked toward his old house. Chino was growing old.

Making them old. Adults.

Theresa looked at him. *Where are we going?*

You'll see. Ryan squeezed her hand gently. His other hand patted the cigarettes in his pocket.

They continued to walk toward his old house, the sun above finally cooling a few degrees.

As they approached, the home just two houses away, Ryan pulled the cigarettes from his pocket.

Theresa looked at each house as they walked along. He knew she knew. That he was taking her back to his old house.

He opened up the pack of cigarettes and pulled out the lucky one.

Theresa let go of Ryan's hand and took a few steps on her own. Ryan's old house just a few feet away now.

Ryan put the lucky cigarette to his mouth and lit it. The tobacco glowed red and he inhaled.

Theresa stopped in front of Ryan's old house and turned back to him.

Ryan inhaled again.

"What are you doing?" she practically screamed as she saw the lit cigarette in his mouth. Smoke billowing into the afternoon sky. "The baby."

"Luck." Ryan smiled, then inhaled again and blew a smoke ring into the air.

"That's not luck," she screamed. "That's death."

"Please," Ryan pleaded, the cigarette slowly burning in his hand. He needed the luck. He wanted this to work. He wanted the happy family to appear in the window. He wanted everything to be perfect. He wanted her to see that things between them were going to work out. That they didn't have to keep pretending. "If we think our lives are bad now . . ." he began recalling the words they used to say to each other when they were younger.

Theresa's face softened. "Imagine what they would be like if we didn't have luck," she finished.

Smoke drifted from Ryan's lips as he drew another breath of luck. He stood back and watched as her face continued to soften and a tear formed in the corner of her eye. Just small enough to get caught there. Unable to escape to the softness of her cheek.

She took a step toward Ryan. He held the cigarette behind his back, allowing the smoke to drift away from them. He didn't want to harm the unborn child.

But Theresa continued to walk toward him. Her face inches apart from Ryan's, he could feel her breath upon his skin. Then she reached behind him and pulled the cigarette from his fingers. And she held it in her own hand and brought it up to Ryan's lips.

Her eyes said everything and he inhaled.

Then she took the cigarette to her own lips, cautiously, and she inhaled.

And they held the smoke inside their mouths. Waiting. Then with each breath they let out they blew tiny smoke rings. And each ring crossed with the other. Ryan's with Theresa's. And as they crossed they disintegrated into one. A ritual they had done since they were young. Since the first time they had tried smoking together.

They blew out the rest of the smoke from their mouths and they looked into each other's eyes.

Ryan dropped the cigarette to the graying sidewalk and put it out with his boot. Theresa reached for his hand and they stood outside the house. Waiting. They had luck. Now all they needed was the sign.

The warm Chino air blew against their backs, and the noise of the neighbors all barbecuing and celebrating echoed down the street. And they waited. Content. All anger and resentment between them gone. All the tension of the summer released.

Until the light in the kitchen of the house went on and Ryan saw the father enter with a basket of food that he placed on the table. The same father he had seen earlier at the store. And he waited for the young mother to appear, baby in hand, and for the two of them to kiss and smile and enjoy the presence of the other.

But when the mother appeared, there was no baby in her arms. Her hair was knotted and dirty and she appeared inebriated. Drunk.

Ryan squeezed Theresa's hands, *why now?* And he wanted to lead her away, but he couldn't. Something kept him there.

The two watched as the once happy family fell apart in front of their eyes. And with each slap, Ryan and Theresa took a step backwards. And with each scream, audible from all the way out here, their hands slowly drifted apart.

Until the two of them could no longer see inside the kitchen, and they stood apart.

Until finally they heard the slamming of the front door and the father running out. Screaming. *I'm leaving.*

Ryan and Theresa walked all the way home in silence. The sign was never a sign. Their luck was never luck. And he coughed up the phlegm of the cigarette, the tainted luck, and thought how ridiculous he had been. He knew how Chino worked. He'd always known.

Dreams did not come true here.

And he thought how jaded he had become, how in just one year he'd gained a false sense of security and hope. That you could get anything if you just put your mind to it. And he thought how this had seemed true in Newport. But now as he stood here walking with Theresa, he knew that

Newport was only a facade, a mask on the life he really had. And he vowed that if he ever got the chance to return, he would make his dreams come true. That he wouldn't take anything for granted. That he would throw himself into the dream.

He reached for Theresa's hand, but she pulled away. And he knew. The young family was never a sign.

They entered Theresa's house in silence.

Her eyes immediately drawn to the roses, she went over and picked another petal. *He loves me not.*

And she held the petal in her hand and went outside to her family. To the party. As Ryan stood alone inside.

And he watched her walk out into the yard and over to her mom, who reached out her arms and held her daughter within them. Squeezing ever so gently. And Ryan watched as Theresa let the rose petal slip from her hands into the dusty grass yard.

On her face, a smile.

Ryan continued to watch as she moved around the yard. Laughing and smiling.

And then he knew for sure. They would continue to pretend. Forever.

That night, Ryan lay awake on the couch. He couldn't sleep. He looked at the roses. *Not.* Then he looked at the window and remembered his brother, how he had come one night and tapped on the very same window and they had tried to escape, but failed. And he thought about the family he once had. The drunken, destructive one he had here, and the one in Newport, his home. And he thought about the family he would never have. And as he fell asleep that night he waited for a tap on the window, someone to come and rescue him and take him home to his family.

The next morning Ryan awoke to find Theresa up and ready to go. His brown-bag lunch in her hands. When he was ready for work, she drove him to the construction site. To the house that wasn't finished. The house that would hopefully be a home.

And as she handed him his lunch and said good-bye, she added "I peeled the orange."

He knew this was how it would be. They would continue on. The paper-bag lunch. The peeled orange. The ride to work. Their ritual of pretense.

12

Marissa woke in DJ's arms. His soft, dark skin tight against her. And she smiled. Ever since she had gone over to his place in tears they had become closer. And she had been spending more and more time there. Sneaking out at night and driving over to see him. Sneaking kisses as she lay out by the pool during the day while her mom and Kaitlin were at yogalates and Caleb was at work. Leaving him notes in the pool house among his equipment.

She looked down at his strong hands, and she breathed in his smell. Comforted by his strength. And she wanted to lie in bed with him forever. But then she remembered, today was the Fourth of July and she had promised Summer that she would spend the day with her.

Marissa tried to inch her way out of the bed, but he awoke and held her tightly as he kissed the back of her head. "Don't go," he whispered.

Marissa rolled over.

"I'm sorry. I promised Summer," she said as she tried to pull away.

"Just a little while," DJ pleaded as he kissed her again, pulling her closer.

"I can't. I have to go."

"Then I'll come with you," he said, loosening his grip and moving with her.

"No," she said sharply and turned on him a bit too quickly.

DJ retreated back to the bed, a hurt look upon his face.

"I mean, it's just . . ." she started, trying to cover. Even though they had grown closer, DJ was still *her* little secret, and hers alone. She didn't want him to meet her friends.

"It's just that you don't want to be seen with the gardener," he retorted angrily.

"No."

"You're just like all of them. You pretend you're not, but you are. Go ahead, sleep with the gardener, break barriers. If that makes you feel like you're not one of them, great. But you are."

"I'm not. And that's the truth. Isn't it more fun keeping this a secret? Sneaking around. Hiding from Caleb?"

"For who?"

"I have to go," she said softly. Knowing DJ was right.

"Fine, I'm working later. Maybe I'll see you. Or maybe not. Since I'm a secret, perhaps I'm invisible as well."

"DJ, please. You know I'd spend all day with

you if I could. Don't make this an issue. I promised Summer. I have to go." She stood up from the bed and put on her shirt.

"Or she'll get suspicious?"

"No, I just promised. I'll see you later."

"Bye," he said and blew her a dismissive kiss.

And Marissa left with the stinging thought that maybe her perfect escape was becoming more, was wanting more. Was he becoming her boyfriend? And what would happen if Ryan returned? What then? Would she run back to him? Or would she have to stay loyal to DJ? Marissa's mind raced as she drove back home.

Marissa crept into her house, trying to avoid her mom or Caleb, but just as she was about to run up the stairs Julie emerged from the kitchen.

"Marissa, what are you doing home? I thought you slept at Summer's so that you could hang out all day today."

"I did, but I forgot the top to my suit," Marissa said quickly, then ran up the stairs.

"If you guys get bored with the beach there'll be plenty of food and people here later. Stop by."

But Marissa kept running up to her room and didn't answer her mother. Caleb and Julie were throwing a Fourth of July party, and Julie had gone overboard on everything. The food. The drink. The music. And the decorations. This was the first party she had gotten to throw in her new mansion and she was ready to show it off. She had invited all of Newport's elite and she was running around frantically trying to make sure everything was perfect.

Upstairs, Marissa quickly changed into her swimsuit and a skirt and was about to run downstairs and over to Summer's when she decided to go out on her balcony.

From there she could see all that her mother had put together for the party. There was a big white tent with tables and chairs and a dance floor. White lights strewn in the trees and on top of the tent. Tables with alternating red and blue flower centerpieces. Red roses and white candles floated in the pool and about twenty workers ran around making sure everything was perfect. There was a long buffet table for the catered food that would arrive later and two bars set up on opposite ends of the backyard. Marissa took it all in, breathing in the warm summer air. She felt distanced, like her backyard had been taken over by a traveling circus. That all the workers would have to pack up and leave, and all the excitement would soon die off. This was not her home. DJ was wrong. She was not one of them.

Summer was growing impatient by the time Marissa arrived at her house.

"Sorry I'm late," Marissa said as she pulled into the driveway to find Summer waiting on the front step. "My mom made me help with her party," she lied.

Summer quickly got into the car. "Fine. Can we go now? Zach's waiting for us."

Marissa started the car and sped away toward Zach's beach house out on the peninsula.

"How's that going, by the way?"

"What? Oh, Zach?" Summer smiled. Marissa nodded.

"What's with you two? Are you together?"

"We're dating, I guess. Except we don't go on many dates. Just hang out on his boat or at his beach house. Mainly we make out a lot."

"So you're kissing, not dating."

"Yes. I don't know. I like him. And besides, he takes my mind off Cohen."

"Has he called again?"

"No."

"Oh," Marissa said, turning back to the road.

"You know, Coop, you should try finding someone. This whole 'kissing' thing really helps you get over someone."

"I don't know," Marissa said reluctantly. "I think I'm over Ryan. He's doing the right thing. I can't be mad at him. And I can't wait around. I'm okay."

"Don't you get horny? You and Ryan used to kiss all the time. Sometimes it was even gross."

"Summer!"

"What? It's true."

"No. I don't get horny." And she thought about DJ. How she had left so abruptly. And she started to feel guilty.

"Oh. Well, I still think you need to find someone."

"I like being alone," Marissa said, making herself hide her secret. Refusing to let on that she wasn't alone. That every night she slept with DJ and woke up in his arms.

She smiled at Summer and faked her happiness. The thought of DJ running through her mind. His warm body next to her. And she wondered if he could be her secret forever. But after this morning she knew things were rocky, that unless she did something it would all come crashing down. Just like secrets always did. Because no matter how bad you want to hold in the truth, someone always leaks it. Marissa thought about her mom and Luke and their secret affair. How Seth and Ryan had caught them and tried to keep it a secret, but how she had eventually found out the truth. And she wondered if the truth about DJ ever came out, if it would hurt as much as when she found out about her mom and Luke sleeping together. And she wondered who would be hurt more: her? Or DJ?

Marissa pulled her car into the driveway behind Zach's house and she and Summer grabbed their towels and headed inside.

Zach's beach house was filled with just about the entire two upper classes of Harbor, plus about twenty or so graduates who had come back from college to live in Newport for the summer.

The two girls made their way through the crowds of people, past girls walking around in skirts and bikini tops, guys wearing nothing but their boardshorts and a pair of Rainbow sandals. It was a sea of blond-haired, blue-eyed, tanned beauty, and Marissa and Summer were caught up in its current.

Summer grabbed Marissa's hand and navigated them through the house and out onto the back patio where more shirtless guys and girls in bikinis were barbecuing and drinking beer. The sandy beach lay just steps away on the other side of the patio. Summer let go of Marissa's hand and ran over to Zach, who was manning the keg.

As soon as he saw her coming, Zach put down the tap and walked over to embrace Summer. She jumped into his arms and he held her tight as he kissed her on the lips. Marissa plastered a smile on her face and joined them.

"Hi, Marissa," Zach said politely as he let go of Summer but moved his hand down to hold her pinky finger with his.

"Hi," Marissa replied just as politely. Then she eyed the untapped keg. The idea of quenching her thirst with the cool beer enticed her. She reached for a cup, but Zach stopped her.

"Hold on. There's a lot of foam right now. I need to adjust the regulator to lower the pressure . . ." Zach twisted the top of the tap. ". . . and then let out some of the carbon dioxide . . ." The keg hissed. Then he reached for a cup. "And voilà. Foamless beer," he finished as he poured the beer into the cup and handed it to Marissa.

Marissa took the cup and sipped gently. She smiled thanks.

"He knows, like, everything," Summer said to

Marissa as Zach turned his back to pour another beer.

Marissa nodded and sipped some more of her beer. Its coolness started to send a buzz through her body. A slight tingle.

Zach turned back around and handed a beer to Summer. Then he held his cup high and held it out for Marissa and Summer to touch with theirs. They held their cups up and the three said cheers. "To Summer," Zach began, "to the barbecues and drinking, and the beauty beside me." Summer smiled and squeezed his hand.

Marissa chugged her beer and thought how cheesy Zach's cheers had been, how unoriginal the play on words was. But as she watched the two of them she grew jealous of their connection. Their intimacy. And she thought again of DJ.

She was torn. She wanted the secret and she wanted the truth. All at once. And she thought how if she didn't live in Newport, she could have both. How she was almost jealous of Ryan that he got to get out of here, but she remembered the reality of it all and realized that the secret was better than facing the real world. A new family. But then she thought of Seth, who could be anywhere, and she was jealous of him. He had escaped and neither she nor Summer knew where he had gone. He had gotten out before things became disastrous. Before they had to spend another summer living the life of the perfect Newporter.

Marissa poured herself another beer as Summer and Zach continued to flirt and kiss each other.

Marissa stood alone. Not talking. Her lips still except when she took another sip of her beer. She let the coldness run through her body, the numbness she had grown so fond of over the summer slowly creeping in, and she began to feel like she belonged. That if she could stay drunk and numb forever then that would be her mask, and she would be able to hide behind its facade and face all of Newport. Even her mother and Caleb. Even the prospect that she would never see or hear from Ryan again.

"Coop, look alive. It's the Fourth," Summer said as she approached.

Marissa took a sip of her beer and shook her head, emerging from her daze.

"Cheers," Marissa said and held out her beer. Summer held hers up and they finished off their cups.

Marissa grabbed Summer's empty cup and went over to the keg to refill them both as Summer stood staring out at the ocean.

"Remember last summer? When we used to hang out by that lifeguard station and watch Luke and Nordlund and Saunders surf," Summer asked as Marissa returned with their beers.

"We were really tan that summer," Marissa replied as she looked down at her arm, its golden glow a reflection of their new summer.

"Do you ever think we'll go back to that?"

"No. Do you?" Marissa asked, knowing the truth. Knowing that they would never go back to that because so much had changed over the last year. In her mind, she'd gotten to leave Newport and the idea of having to return still did not register with her. Even as she stood here among half of Harbor High and its alumni, she didn't feel like she'd completely returned. She'd had Ryan and he'd shown her life outside of Newport. It was like showing a kid their dessert and letting them taste it, then telling them that they could no longer have it, that they had to suffer through Brussels sprouts before they could ever even get a glimpse of their dessert again. And Marissa wasn't ready for Brussels sprouts. She'd rather stay drunk in purgatory with DJ than return to the wretched vegetable if she wasn't allowed to be with Ryan. If she'd never see him again.

"I guess we've grown up a lot this summer. Couldn't really see us going back to that. We went through a lot. Losing your first love? That's huge. Getting over that love? Even bigger. I would say it's a good thing that you and I won't go back to pining over the bad boys and the Cohens of this world," Summer said.

"And you've got Zach," Marissa added, gulping beer, feeling even more out of place.

"And you've got . . ." Summer paused, realizing that she'd said the wrong thing. She put her arm around Marissa. "But you know what? We've got each other."

Marissa smiled at her friend. *Yeah, we've got each other.* Then she watched as Summer walked back into the house to find Zach, and Marissa stood alone on the back patio watching the rest of Newport enjoy the holiday. The happy couples walking hand in hand along the beach. The guys playing volleyball in the sand. The girls gossiping in their bikinis as their hair became blonder and their skin darker. And Marissa continued to sip her beer until her cup was empty.

She looked back at the house to see if Summer was ready to go or if she wanted to go for a walk down the beach to the pier to see what else was going on, but inside Summer was distracted. Her hand glued to Zach's.

So Marissa took her cup and filled it up with beer, then sipped off the top so that it wouldn't spill and she walked out onto the warm summer sand. The wind blew at her hair and she continued to walk until she reached the water's edge. She stood there sipping her beer as cool ocean waves lapped at her feet. Each wave brought more sand and her feet began to form indentations, then holes, and soon she was up to her ankles in cold wet sand, but she didn't care. She wondered if she stood here long enough, could she disappear? Perhaps her whole body would be covered in sand and she could disappear forever. The waves continued to break against her legs, and her body shook with numbness; the beer was affecting her, leaving her unstable. The tide rushed in and each wave became stronger. Tighter. More binding. And Marissa began to believe that she really could disappear and she wondered if anyone would notice. If she became one with the sand and she ceased to exist, would the world notice? Would Newport care?

Marissa swallowed the last drop of her beer and placed the plastic cup in the sand next to her. An SOS. A message in a bottle. *Save me.* And she watched as each wave lapped against it, slowly pulling it out to sea, and she wanted to be that bottle and she wanted to follow it, but she knew she couldn't. Finally a wave caught her unaware, knocking her off her feet. She dropped to her knees, kneeling in the sand, wet and cold.

Finally, she forced herself to stand and Marissa trudged back to Zach's house, shivering with cold and defeat. She couldn't stay here any longer.

She found Summer with Zach and she pleaded with them to let her leave. She was cold and wet and she wanted to go back to her house, to Caleb's mansion high up on the hill. At least there she had a room that she could call her own. A retreat. With some convincing and coaxing, Summer finally let her leave and she got in her car and drove back to Caleb's, through the massive holiday traffic and the crowds of people and the blocked-off streets. By the time she got back to the top of the hill, the sun was beginning to cool and the day was coming to a close.

Marissa pulled up the driveway to find it packed with cars. A valet stepped out and offered to park her car for her. "I live here," Marissa said unconvincingly. "I'll put it in the garage." But the valet did not believe her and Marissa finally had to pull out the garage door opener and prove herself to the young man who was just trying to do his job. *Sorry.* She winked, then put her car away.

She dragged her cold, wet body out of her car and into the house. Inside was like a library compared to the mass chaos out in the backyard. Marissa quietly walked up the stairs. A tiny trail of sand followed her to her room.

The warm water of the shower ran over her shaking body, the numbness from the cold and the beer slowly subsiding. The sand washing down the drain. As each grain drifted away she was another step farther from burying herself in the sea, another step away from disappearing forever. Then she felt the tears form in her eyes and she wanted to scream. Let the whole world hear that she was aching, that she wanted out of this house, that she wanted her family back, that she wanted to just be herself, and she wanted to fold up in Ryan's arms and let him protect her. But she couldn't scream; the warm water held her back and the tears continued to flow and she sank down into the bottom of the shower and let the water beat on her back as she held her knees close to her chest, rocking back and forth with each tiny cry for help. She wondered if things would ever go back to being normal, or at least tolerable. She missed the days when Newport didn't bother her. Before she had crossed to the other side, before she had realized that there was more outside Newport than what was contained inside the tiny bubble her parents had made for her. And she wanted Ryan to come back and she wanted to wear Pucci and her new Chanel outfit, and she wanted to feel like she could do anything, that no matter what she felt or thought or said or did, she would not be judged. That there were no standards to live up to. No Newport code of living. No debutante balls to attend and no social committee to chair. The cold and the numbness continued to retreat with the tears and the warm water pounding on her back and she wanted to run, but she had nowhere to go. No escape except the bottle and DJ. And both had become a part of who she was. A part of the girl she had become, and so Marissa slowly lifted herself from the depths of the shower and turned off the water. She toweled herself dry and wiped the tears from her face.

Then she went into her room and found the box with all the alcohol and she pulled out an anonymous bottle and began to slowly sip its contents. The numbness returned and her tears began to dry. Her heartbeat slowed. Now she was in control. The mask was hers to take on and off. And DJ, she knew, was just beyond the balcony, cleaning up after the sea of Newporters who swarmed the backyard.

So she stood in front of the sheer white drapes, sending a signal to DJ — to see if he would respond.

Then she drifted to her closet and put on some

clothes. Her wet hair stuck to her face and her neck and she pulled it back out of the way as she moved back to the balcony doors and opened them. Outside she could hear voices rising and falling in shrill laughter, masking their fears. The fear that one day they would be found out. That one day they, too, would feel like Marissa. She took a deep breath and spit out the last bit of air as she searched for DJ.

When she spotted him, she trained her eyes upon him. Hoping. Willing. That he would take the chance and look up. That he would feel her desire and turn around.

And when he did, Marissa waved with just one finger, inched it back toward herself, then pointed to a door on the side of the house. DJ shook his head no, but Marissa insisted. Kept her gaze upon him and seduced him with her needs.

Downstairs, Marissa found DJ waiting just where she had directed him to go and she pulled him inside the house.

"We shouldn't. . . ."

But she placed her lips upon his and he was silent. "I'm sorry," she whispered. Then she quickly led him up to her room and shut the door behind them.

She pushed him onto the bed and began to pull at his clothes. DJ hesitated for a moment. Looking at the door. Should they do this? But Marissa kissed him gently on the neck and he kissed her back.

They moved closer and closer, as they kissed

more and more. DJ was shirtless, his muscles rippling and tan from the day in the sun. She placed his arms around her and felt the comfort seep into her body. Let it mix with the numbness, and she was high. She hadn't felt this free since the first time she had kissed Ryan and she knew things would never be the same.

That maybe someday she would have to admit her secret, but until then she would continue to pursue him. She kissed his chest, his muscles hard against her lips, and she thought they could go on forever.

Until the door opened wide and Marissa knew she had been caught. And she was terrified to turn around, afraid to face the wrath of her mother or Caleb.

But when she finally turned, she found herself face-to-face with Kaitlin.

"What are you — ?" Marissa screeched as she jumped up from her bed.

"I'm sorry . . . I just came to borrow that necklace. The gold one you were going to let me —" Kaitlin stammered.

Marissa went to the dresser and threw the necklace at her little sister. "I thought Mom said it looked hideous. Aren't you like her mini protégé? What if she catches you?"

And Kaitlin looked as though she were going to burst into tears. DJ inched his way to the edge of the bed and slowly, quietly began to put his shirt back on. But Kaitlin's face changed. A new sense of confidence came over her. "What did she ever do to you?" Kaitlin asked with force.

"You want to know?" Marissa screamed. "You really want to know?" And now Marissa was furious and almost in tears. This was the first time she had ever gotten this angry over all that her mother had done to her. "She —" But she couldn't say it. As much as she wanted to be vengeful and spite her mother, she couldn't hurt her little sister. She couldn't shatter her perfect world just as her own had been shattered. And so she held back. Didn't tell Kaitlin that their mom had slept with Luke, her ex-boyfriend.

But now Kaitlin was irate and demanded, "She what?"

"Don't you ever get sick of it? Mimicking her? Becoming the next Julie Cooper? Doesn't that scare you? Don't you want to be your own person?"

"Like you?" Kaitlin asked. "I know what you're doing. That box." And Kaitlin pointed to the box full of alcohol. "You're just like them. They hide, too."

"I'm not hiding," Marissa said as she picked up a pillow and threw it at the door. "What do you know? You're eleven."

"I know that I'm getting out of Newport before I turn out like either of you."

Marissa said nothing. Her sister was right. "Please don't . . ."

"I won't tell." And with that, Kaitlin walked out the door.

DJ stood up from the bed and started to walk to the door, but Marissa stopped him. "Don't go."

DJ hesitated. "Maybe you should be alone." And he turned again to walk away but Marissa grabbed his wrist.

"I should be with you." Then she kissed him and let the smell and taste of him intoxicate her like the alcohol did. "Let's get out of here," she whispered.

And DJ led her down the stairs and out the side door and around to the side of the house and down the hill where his car was parked.

"Am I really like them?" she asked. The thought reverberating in her head. Blocking the numbness.

"No," DJ said as he looked into her eyes and began to kiss her. "You're Marissa."

Then she lay back in his bed and let his strength comfort her.

Her alcohol buzz slowly faded and she accepted that she would always be from Orange County. That she could never really escape Newport. Even if she had to live in secret. In an empty house.

13

A stack of letters piled upon the desk. Fifty sheets of white paper all neatly stacked one on the other. One for every time he had missed Summer. But Seth hadn't been able to send them.

Dear Summer, he wrote, but today he couldn't go much further. Something in him had changed. He still missed her. But he couldn't write the same letter again. He couldn't tell her that he would be home soon, because he wasn't sure that this was true anymore.

After his mom called a few days ago and he'd refused to go back to Newport, he knew that things were different. He thought about calling his mom, apologizing, telling her that he wasn't mad at her, that it wasn't personal, but that without Ryan and Summer Newport didn't really offer him anything. He didn't feel like he was a part of the city.

Seth put the unfinished letter on top of the stack. The whiteness staring at him. A change. Then Seth went to his sketchbook and pulled out the last drawing he had done. The one of the comic book character of Summer that he had been working on during his trip to Astoria with Cali.

The fierce Summer stood staring at him. The sexiness of her superhero outfit tight against her pencil-drawn body.

He placed the drawing on top of the stack.

But he couldn't say good-bye.

He still missed her.

So he took the stack of papers and placed them under his mattress. Pressing them between the box spring and the mattress, still holding them close, but placing them out of reach.

Today was the Fourth of July, and Seth was still in Portland. Newport would be packed. The police would have shut down the streets near the beaches and stopped allowing cars onto the peninsula. His parents would be getting ready for the party at Caleb's.

He picked up the phone.

He still felt bad for hanging up on his mom. An apology was owed. His fingers moved across the keypad, dialing the nine-four-nine number, the one ingrained in his head. He would say he was sorry.

But when the voice picked up on the other end, he didn't recognize it. Not at first. A million thoughts flooded his mind. Was his mom having an affair? Did his dad leave? Is that why she wanted him to come back to Newport?

"Hello," the voice said again. Only this time Seth recognized it.

The voice was Summer's dad.

"Hello?" he said again.

And Seth stood still and speechless. The voice kept saying hello. Finally, Seth hung up the phone.

It was a sign, he thought. A sign that he needed time. He wasn't supposed to call home. He wasn't supposed to call Summer. Not yet.

He still had a plan. A plan to find his home. And he needed time.

Seth put on his boardshorts and T-shirt and was about to head downstairs when there was a knock on his door.

"Let's go, Cohen," Luke said as he opened the door.

"I'm coming," Seth said as he turned and saw that Jane and Amanda were standing there with Luke, in their bikini tops and shorts. "Very quickly," he finished.

"We're teaching you how to ski," Jane said.

"Luke said you needed to learn if you were going to stay in Portland," Amanda added.

Seth grabbed his towel and nodded. The thoughts of Summer and Newport and Ryan and his mom slowly fading. He would have to learn how to waterski if he was going to stay in Portland.

"Thumbs-up means faster. Thumbs-down, slower. The okay sign means perfect, and this," Jane said as she slid her hand across her throat, making a slicing motion, "means you've had enough."

Seth nodded, then buckled his life jacket and hopped into the water. His skin shivered. Even for the middle of the summer, the water was quite cold.

"No one told me the water'd be this cold."

"Cohen, you sail. You've been in the water every day since you got here," Luke yelled.

"My point exactly. I sail. I don't swim."

"Just put your skis on and let's go." Jane laughed as she threw the tow-rope out to Seth.

Experience, Seth thought as his teeth chattered. *It's all about the experience.* Seth slid his feet into the skis and held tight to the rope.

"Okay," he screamed, then made the okay sign.

The water rushed around him as the boat pulled his body forward and within seconds he was skiing. Skiing. The wind and the spray of the wake whipped through his hair and he felt free. Liberated. He liked this.

He gave the thumbs-up and Luke hit the gas. Seth felt himself being pulled forward, but he kept his balance and continued to ski. Until Luke started whipping the boat back and forth and in circles, forcing Seth outside the wake, where the water was rough and choppy. Until Seth lost his grip and went skidding across the water. Skis flying everywhere.

When Seth got back on the boat, Jane gave him a hug and congratulated him on a job well done. Seth felt a rush surge through his body and he held on to her a second too long. Her warm skin pressing against his.

She pulled away and smiled at him, and Seth smiled back.

He still missed Summer, but was it so bad to flirt with someone while he figured out where he was going next? Whether or not he was going to stay in Portland or return to Newport.

He flicked his towel at her playfully.

"Hey," she said in a sweet voice through a big smile.

"It's just a little game I like to play called flirtation. Have you heard of it?" Seth smiled.

Jane winked and nodded. She liked his games.

For the rest of the afternoon, the two flirted while Luke and Amanda grew closer, constantly kissing.

"Hey, you guys going to come up for air ever?" Seth asked jokingly.

"Very funny," Luke said as he moved away from Amanda, acting like he'd had enough of her, then grabbed her again and pulled her in for a kiss.

"What about you two?" Amanda asked.

"What about us?" Seth asked.

"You going to kiss her or what?"

Seth hesitated. He liked the flirting. But if he kissed her then that would mean the end of him and Summer. Forever. And he wasn't sure he was ready to accept that. Not if there was still a possibility that he would have to go back to Newport.

Jane waited for his response. But he did nothing.

"I have this thing, in my mouth. This sore. Pretty gross. And it hurts. Especially when you get something salty on it. And you don't want that. You have to be in the water every day. With all the salt. Not good."

"Yeah, gross," Jane said softly.

Seth saw her hurt, but he wasn't ready. Not yet.

"Who's up for a little boat racing?" Luke said, saving Seth from the awkward situation.

The girls both shouted yes and ran to the front of the boat.

Seth and Luke took turns driving. Flying past all the other boats and enjoying the cool breeze against their faces.

Whipping up and down the waterways. Spraying wake on other boaters.

And as they raced around in their boat, joking and laughing and enjoying the summer sun, Seth realized why he couldn't call home or Summer.

He was already home. And he couldn't return to Newport.

He was ready to choose.

Seth's plan had worked. He'd opened himself up to experience and let in all these new people. And he'd found his home: Portland.

The fire pit in Luke's backyard grew warm and hot with red and gold. They were cooking s'mores again and waiting for the big fireworks display to happen.

Everyone had changed out of their bathing suits and wet clothes and into sweatshirts and shorts. The night air was chilly.

Seth stood behind Jane, helping her roast her marshmallows. His hands on top of hers. Their faces inches apart. The heat passing between their bodies.

Tonight, he thought, when the fireworks went off they would kiss. It would be like that *Brady Bunch* episode where Jan saw fireworks every time she kissed that special boy. And Seth thought how romantic that would be if when he kissed Jane, there were actual fireworks going off in the background. Their lips were bound to produce fireworks then.

Jane pulled her crisp marshmallow out of the fire and fed it to Seth.

The marshmallow ooze moved down his face. He stuck out his tongue and licked it, the sugary sweetness enveloping him.

There would definitely be fireworks later.

The night sky had turned to black. Just the light of the stars and the moon hovered above them. Illuminating their faces while the light of the fire kept them warm.

All four sat around the fire. Seth's and Jane's fingers interlaced. Luke's arm draped around Amanda. The crackling of the fire was the only sound between them. After spending the day together their conversations had finally lulled. The sun and the day on the water had them all exhausted.

"Where are the fireworks? I need a nap," Luke said, putting his head down on Amanda's shoulder.

"You know what we should do?" Amanda said, pulling Luke's head off her shoulder. Seth and Jane looked at her, *what?* "Skinny dipping," Amanda suggested.

"I do not want to see Cohen naked," Luke gasped.

"Hey, I take offense at that. I work out."

"Hoisting a sail does not count," Luke said.

"Well, I'm going in," Amanda said as she jumped up from her seat and ran toward the water.

"Me too," Jane said as she ran after her.

"They're not really going to —" Seth started, then looked out and saw the girls flinging their clothes off and running into the water. "Yes they are." Seth turned back to Luke. "I'll go first. You can come in once I'm in the water. I won't look if you don't."

"Fine," Luke said, turning his back so that Seth could run to the water and take off his clothes.

"I'm coming in," Seth shouted. "Move over, Nemo, I've found home."

The girls giggled and splashed in the water as Seth approached, his clothes flying to the ground.

And he ran into the cool water, but against the cold air of the night, the water felt warm and refreshing. Seth had never been skinny dipping before and it was kind of liberating.

"Luke, your turn," Seth yelled, then turned his back so that he was facing out into the water. Looking at all the anchored boats. Waiting for the fireworks.

Seth could hear Luke running into the water, the little ripples from his splashing rolled by Seth's arms.

"You in yet?" Seth asked.

"Yeah," Luke yelled as he splashed water at the back of Seth's head.

"You're messing up my Jew fro," Seth said as he turned around and splashed water back at Luke.

"Hey," Amanda screamed and joined in the splashing.

Water sprayed everywhere. And then it became an all-out war. All four splashing and kicking water at the others. A mountain of water cascading all around them. And soon, it became two against two, Seth and Jane versus Luke and Amanda. Fighting. Splashing.

Then an explosion. A loud boom echoed through the night sky. And the water stopped falling. Spraying. The four paused and looked up.

The fireworks had started. Red and blue and white sparkled in the sky.

The four stood watching, until the coldness overtook them and Luke and Amanda made their way to shore and bundled up in their clothes.

Seth and Jane stood in the water up to their necks. Still watching. Moving closer until their faces were just inches away from each other. The fireworks still exploding.

And just as they were about to kiss, Seth heard someone shouting his name. Over the sounds of the exploding fireworks. He heard it. *Seth*. He looked back at Luke but his mouth was occupied. He and Amanda were kissing. Seth looked back to Jane, thinking it was nothing. But as he leaned in to kiss her, he heard the voice again. *Cohen*. He pulled away from Jane. The fireworks still exploding in the background. Then another. *Seth*. And the bright white light from the explosion lit the beach area and Seth saw the source of the voice.

It was Cali.

She'd returned.

Without even thinking, Seth came running out of the water and into the arms of Cali.

"You're wet," she screamed, then looked down, "and naked."

Seth looked down and realized that he was completely exposed. He had totally forgotten that he wasn't wearing any clothes. He put his hands down and attempted to cover himself. Then Luke tossed some clothes at him.

"Thanks," Seth said softly as he quickly got dressed.

Cali stood with a smirk on her face, laughing to herself.

Once Seth was dressed he turned back to the water, quickly realizing that he had left Jane there all alone. But she was nowhere in sight.

Seth panicked. He had left another girl without an explanation. She was going to hate him.

The fireworks continued to burst in the sky. Shedding bits of light on the water and the yard.

Then he saw her. Sopping wet. Holding her clothes tight against her body.

"Wait here," he whispered to Cali, then went to Jane.

"I'm sorry," he said as he approached her. Sorry

that he hadn't kissed her. But even more sorry that he'd just left her in the water so that he could go see another girl.

"It's okay, I understand," she replied quietly, obviously not pleased.

"It's just, I haven't seen —" Seth tried to explain. Tell her that Cali was just a friend.

"It's okay. Really, I'm just going to go —"

"Don't go. I . . ." And he was about to tell her that he liked her but he couldn't bring himself to do it.

"Stay," another voice added to the argument. It was Cali, standing behind Seth. "Please."

Jane hesitated and Seth gave her his best smile, the one that said *please stay*.

"Okay, but on one condition."

"Anything," Seth said.

"Someone get me a warm towel!" She shivered.

Once everyone had dried off and gotten dressed, the five new friends sat around the fire watching the end of the fireworks. Exploding and fading into the night sky.

Five unlikely friends under the stars and the explosions in the air. And Seth was finally happy. Comfortable.

He looked at Cali, who was sitting next to him.

"Why did you come back?" he whispered.

"I'm leaving again. Just needed a quick stop home." She winked at Seth and he smiled.

He knew exactly what she meant.

14

Dear Summer,
Sorry if my mom made you sit through a takeout din-
ner to get this, but I couldn't see you. I had to go.

The sun rose over three different worlds. And three friends trying to find their way.

I've left on the Summer Breeze *and I don't know*
where I'm going, but I've got my sextant (not what
you think!) and a compass.

Ryan awoke to find Theresa up and ready to go. His brown-paper-bag lunch in her hands. Another day of work. Another day of pretending. But he knew he had to keep on, that the baby was another minute closer to arriving.

I don't belong in Newport. The only thing that's
ever kept me here (besides my parents) is you.

Marissa awoke in the arms of DJ. She breathed him in and accepted her fate. Living in secret. Continuing the lifelong lie.

Since the third grade I've had a plan to leave this city. That one day you and I would set sail on this boat.

Seth awoke next to the smoldering fire to find Jane and Cali both gone. The party had ended. He went inside and fell back asleep with the letters to Summer under his mattress. Close, yet far away.

Together we'd get out of here. And believe me when I say this, if I could, I would've taken you with me today. But I couldn't.

They were three worlds apart.

I had to do this on my own.

Ryan in Chino. Pretending.
Marissa in Newport. Escaping.

One day we'll go sailing.

Seth in Portland. Living.

But for now, it's good-bye.

All searching for a home.

I love you Summer. I always have.

Love,
Seth